BOYFRIEND FROM HELL

A TAINTED LOVE NOVELLA

SEDONA JESSIE

Book Cover by Charlotte Slegers

Editing (Developmental & Line) and formatting by Bibliobean Books

Inside Graphics by Sedona Jessie & Bibliobean Books

Proofreading by Sarah Detrich

First edition 2025

Paperback ISBN: 979-8-9985133-2-9

Alt. Cover ISBN: 979-8-9985133-3-6

E-Book ISBN: 979-8-9985133-1-2

"Once you know what my love's gonna feel like, nothing else will feel right."
Benson Boone

Prologue

Raios

"I'M SORRY THAT YOU feel that way, really, but there's nothing I can do about it. I'm working late and won't be back until tomorrow morning at the earliest." The man said on the other line, "Just toss whatever's left in the fridge for me."

"But—" she whispered, her voice small and wavering.

"But what? You like living rent free, right? Roof over your head? The freedom to write those stories that never sell? Let me work. Put whatever crap you made into the fridge. I'll see you when I get home."

Click.

I grunted in disgust at what I was watching, my whole body tensed at the tone he had used with her.

"Fucking prick," I mumbled under my breath as I watched the girl place her phone down on the counter next to the stack of dishes she had pulled to set the table.

I bit the inside of my cheek as I watched her crumble and sink to the kitchen floor, her head dropping into her hands as she cried in silence. I focused on her, willing my mind to pry into hers. I had been watching her, time and time again, mentally bend and fold for the shitty man she called her boyfriend. This was the sixth time he had promised to come home to her after work, only to bail and feign some excuse about needing to stay late or spend one more night out of town.

Piss poor excuse after piss poor excuse. She had no idea what he was really doing behind her back—*I* did, and it made me want to strip the skin from his bones and feed him to the crows. I reached behind me to grab one of the blankets from my bed, not wanting to watch another second of this girl's heart shatter any further. I threw the blanket over the mirror that I had become accustomed to using to peer into the broken woman's life.

"Fuck this," I said out loud to no one. I couldn't just sit there and continue to watch that girls' life fall apart at the seams because of that asshole.

Something had to be done.

Chapter 1

Deer

I always liked to think I was the girl that had everything figured out. That I was *lucky*. That I had the perfect best friend, the perfect boyfriend, the perfect life.

Okay, maybe that last part was a lie, also maybe not necessarily the *perfect* boyfriend. I recently got dumped. Four years down the drain because he just *'couldn't see a future with me'*. Rough, I know.

Anyway, all of that was about to change on my twenty-fifth birthday.

Let's just say falling for my hot-as-sin neighbor after a quick one-night stint wasn't exactly what I wished for when I blew out my metaphorical birthday candles.

Okay, let's start from the beginning—

In my last moments of being twenty-four, I hummed *'happy birthday'* quietly to myself as I opened the lid of the to-go container, beyond eager to dig into the long-awaited treat. I peeled back the wrapper of the cupcake, not caring about the crumbs that fell onto the comforter, *that* would be tomorrow's problem. The moment my lips hit the sweet buttercream icing; it was pure bliss. I swear, a sweet treat could fix almost any problem.

I glanced behind me at the digital clock on my nightstand, seven forty-three pm. Wow, time really flew when you were wallowing in self-pity. I stretched an arm behind me, reaching for the curtain of the window that sat just above my dark, polyester tufted headboard. My shoulder screamed at the angle I was forcing my arm into, but no part of me wanted to adjust my position. I was comfy and God forbid I get myself *uncomfy*. There was supposed to be a meteor shower tonight, which sounded cool in theory, but living in a bigger city—I highly doubted I'd get to see much more than a few streaks in the sky.

After the break up, I couldn't bear the thought of running into Felix on the street or at the coffee shop we used to frequent together. There were only so many times I could Instacart and DoorDash my weekly needs before I had to face the fact that I needed to move. Portland seemed like my best bet—far enough from Felix, and close enough to my best friend. Honestly, anywhere would have been good enough so long as it distanced me from any possibility of running into my ex.

Part of me wanted to hold on. Hold onto that ache, the pain, the hope that maybe if I *did* run into him, all of our problems would wash away and he'd take me back. I knew deep down those thoughts and feelings weren't healthy and were only tearing new holes through my already wounded heart. Plus, he made it *very* clear how he felt about me, when he said he 'couldn't see a future with me'.

Yea, distance was beyond necessary.

Distance from the ghost of him, from the places we'd been, the memories that clung to every streetlight and hung on every breeze. My move was hasty and sloppy (which was putting it lightly). I snagged the first studio apartment I could find that was within my budget, and well—let's just say, you really do get what you pay for.

After a moment of struggle, I finally managed to clutch the thin fabric I'd been reaching for—damn near dislocating my shoulder in the process—between my fingertips and flick it aside. The metal rings whispered along the rod, revealing the clear night sky behind it. At least I had a decent view—no buildings blocked my line of sight. I crammed a chunk of the small cake in my mouth, balled up the wrapper and tossed it onto the floor beside me, then licked a glob of icing off my fingertip—when suddenly, I was assaulted by an all-too-high-pitched trill that screamed from down the hall. That was my best friend Gracie's ringtone, the sudden noise caused me to jump, and even worse, to drop the cupcake onto my comforter.

"Gah! Dammit!" I clenched my jaw in frustration and let out a sigh instead of screeching over the fallen treat. This space was too small for a washer and dryer, which meant I'd have to haul it to the closest laundromat—*or* try to hand-wash the icing out in my tub. (Spoiler, I'd be hand-washing it in the tub).

A groan of annoyance and frustration rushed from me as my phone continued to scream. Can I seriously not have anything nice? The sound was like a wailing siren—Gracie had chosen her own ringtone, a perfectly irritating, unignorable tone, because heaven forbid, I missed her calls. Who am I kidding, she's my best friend, it's not like I would ever *actually* ignore her (but she could have chosen a less irritating ringtone).

My heartbeat rose to my ears as the ring continued to slice through the peace and quiet previously surrounding me. The pounding muffled the screeching sound that permeated through the room a tiny bit, my anxiety spiking as if it couldn't decide if I was being hunted for sport or just listening to a phone ring.

I unwound my legs and the moment my feet hit the floor a sudden irrational fear that something was waiting to drag me beneath the bed fired through my brain. Getting used to living solo was going to be a whole chore.

Thanks, anxiety.

The melancholy, unending ring on the other end of the line felt as though it lasted a lifetime. He didn't even have his voicemail set up, which made it all the more mortifying because that meant my attempted call could theoretically go on for as long as I felt desperate enough to allow.

I chewed the inside of my lip, nibbling at the small bit of fatty tissue as the soundwaves engraved themselves into the folds of my brain. Worry used to lace my veins when he didn't answer my calls, but now a sobering, weighted blanket of sadness just wound itself around my heart. He'd never answer my calls again.

I pressed the button on the side of my phone, ending the call and not bothering to look at the log of minutes showing on the screen shortly before it went dark—an unnecessary reminder of how long I sat there waiting for him to pick up—and placed my phone face down on the table in front of me. I stole a glance at my friend who sat across from me, her face a mix of amusement and pity—but mostly amusement, that made me self-conscious. Like I was a spectacle.

My stomach twisted and I averted my gaze from hers. I honestly didn't know why I even bothered to call, especially in front of Gracie. Part of me hoped he would actually answer but another, much more rational part of me, knew it was foolish of me to even hope. If it wasn't for her encouragement for me to see if he'd be willing to drive up the last few boxes of my things, I probably wouldn't have even bothered.

"No answer?" A soft voice cut through the wall of sadness that had begun to close in around me.

I lifted my eyes and met Gracie's gaze again—this time, the blatant amusement was gone, replaced by a quiet understanding I hadn't seen before. There was no way she could ever understand what this felt like. To my knowledge she'd been with the same guy since high school, I doubted she'd ever even experienced heartbreak. And if she had, she sure as hell never said anything to me about it.

Men always seemed to pine after her—*perfect, Gracie.* Whereas I always felt like I had to sell myself like a prize pony, hoping to land a semi-decent man.

I silently wondered if I should send him a follow up text, but quickly decided against it. I already called him five times in the last forty-eight hours leading up to my birthday (but we don't need to talk about that).

If Gracie and her boyfriend ever broke up, I bet he would have brought her things to her if she moved out. No. Her boyfriend—*fiancé* rather—damn near worshiped the ground she walked on. Hell would freeze over before either of them even considered breaking up.

I shrugged it off. "Probably busy—a meeting or something," I mumbled and grabbed the lukewarm chai that sat in front of me beside my phone.

Gracie sighed and reached her hand out toward mine; her perfect porcelain fingers grazed my skin before she delicately laced them around my wrist. I couldn't help but avert my eyes as the gargantuan emerald-cut rock weighing down her ring finger flashed in the soft café light.

"I don't know why you ever put up with him to begin with. He's an asshole—he's always *been* an asshole. This break up aside, this isn't even the first birthday of yours he's missed. What boyfriend—what *man*—can't even be bothered to pick up his phone for his woman on her birthday?"

"I'm not his woman anymore." Saying the words out loud made me feel small, tears burning at the corners of my eyes just from voicing them.

Gracie scoffed. "*Regardless,* Deer. I don't care if you guys just broke up—the least he could do, if he's going to be that big of a dick and not even wish you a happy birthday, is offer to help you move. I mean, it's not like you have a car. Work or not, what if it was an emergency, you know?" She huffed again, saying everything as if he still cared about me.

There was a break in her words, giving me a moment to blink the tears that threatened to spill from my eyes back. She wasn't wrong, if the tables had been turned, I would have likely still wished Felix a happy birthday or at the very least, if he had called several times, reached out to see what was up.

"Do you still have a lot of things at his place?"

I shook my head—a lie. I definitely had *a lot* of things still there. When I moved out, I mainly brought my essentials—things I couldn't survive without, which ended up only being a handful of boxes. Kind of sad, really.

Everything I had left behind, I already mentally said goodbye to and assumed I'd never see again.

Gracie sighed and reached her other hand across the table to rest both hands on mine, rubbing her thumbs across my skin. "I'm sorry. I'm not good at breakups, too many rom-coms. I guess I just figured since you guys were together for so long he'd at least, I don't know, be less sucky? Do you think he's already moved on?"

Uh, ouch? Her question felt like a slap to the face.

"I don't know?" I scrunched my face up at the question. It completely caught me off guard. I assumed (hoped) if he was too busy to be around for me when we *were* together (him not seeing a future with me aside) that meant he *also* didn't have time for anyone else.

She mumbled something under her breath I couldn't quite hear, not that I particularly *wanted* to hear it. I wanted to skirt the topic of my ex already moving on as fast as humanly possible. Why would she even care if he moved on already, anyway? It's not like he's *her* ex.

I sighed. I knew she was just being a good friend and looking out for me, as any best friend would, but the words still stung all the same. Breakups are never easy, I would know. Every man I'd ever been with left me for one piss-poor reason or another. Maybe I'm the problem. Maybe I'm just purely unlovable. I shook my head, keeping my eyes locked on the taupe-colored liquid in my mug. I could feel the familiar sting of tears in my eyes, but I'll be damned if I let myself cry again. Not that I didn't *want* to cry, just not here. Hell, I wanted nothing more than to curl up in a weeping ball and wail. But I couldn't do that here—especially not in front of Gracie. What I really wanted to do was rip my heart from my chest and throw it under an oncoming bus just to rid myself of the thing all together.

Gracie retracted her hands and scoffed; I didn't need to look at her to know that my best friend's face was twisted in her signature beautiful scowl.

"I know exactly what you need!"

Reluctantly, I looked up at her and groaned at the familiar scheming sound of her voice.

"You need to forget about that asshat and go out! You're in a new city—a new city that *I* just so happen to live in and know all the best clubs. What do you say?"

How am I supposed to answer that? Am I supposed to confess I'm desperate and wished he'd text me back saying this was all a sick joke and he wants me back? Or that I'd rather sit in the dark and stare at my phone, waiting for his name to pop up? Admit I'm weak and don't actually want to move on or even try to? Acknowledge I have some type of deep-seated low self-worth that only a therapist could help me with?

Pass.

I haul my mug to my lips. "It's only been six months," I state dryly before I sip my now cold drink.

A snort escapes my friend. "Yea six months post-Felix, but be real, Deer. It's not like he was ever there to begin with. Sure, he's hot-ish, but besides that he doesn't have anything going for him! He was always leaving you to go on work trips, *he was barely around to begin with."*

I made a face at her at the mention of him being hot-*ish*. She wasn't wrong—he'd been absent in almost every way throughout the entirety of our relationship. But still, I wasn't *alone-alone.* It was true though; he was never really present for me. He *did* pay my bills while we lived together and that was pretty ideal. For an aspiring author, it was honestly the most ideal really—if you looked at it, closed one eye and squinted the other, it was perfect. But the lonely nights vastly outweighed the nights where he was home in any capacity.

Four years ago, at the start of our relationship, he had been perfect. Doting on me, taking me on romantic dates, toe-curling sex. He was more than hot-ish to me. He was everything. I had been head over heels for him, so of course when he asked me to move in—with the promise of taking care of me and someday making me his wife—no shit, I said yes. Who wouldn't have?

I was just starting my career as an independent author after being rejected by hundreds of agents. Bills paid, rent free life with a hot man? Sign me up! But then, it all came to an end—of course—as all my relationships did. He was offered a promotion at work in year two of our relationship, and that's when the distance between us really showed itself.

In the beginning, he would make it a point to call me every night, no matter the time zone. Video chat, text, email—whatever he could do to stay in contact with me, he did. But then it started with a missed call, then it became *"I worked late and crashed early"* texts, then came the missed calls and no texts at all. Honestly, if it wasn't for the continuous flow of money into the account he had set up for me when I first moved in, coupled with the fact the lights were still working in his house, I would have thought the man died.

"Deer?" Gracie nudged my foot under the table with hers, "Hello? Earth to Deer—"

I lowered my mug, snapping back to reality. "Sorry, what?"

"I asked if you wanted to go to the quarry with Vince and I? A few of his work friends are getting together to watch the meteor shower tonight." She leaned forward, resting her elbows on the table. "It could be fun! I can even swing by the bakery after this and snag a cake. We could turn it into a little impromptu birthday party."

A birthday party with strangers? Why not just buy me a sweater and stitch 'pathetic' onto the chest and parade me around town.

"Oh, uh—"

"His coworkers are so nice, kind of nerdy, you know, *coders* or whatever—but they're super welcoming. And, I'd make sure it wasn't weird or anything," Gracie pressed, looking at me with expectant, wide eyes. "Plus, the new guy is single! They just hired him. I don't know much about him, but when I visited Vince at work the other day, I *did* catch a glimpse of him—he's hot, with a capital 'H'."

Great, she's already playing matchmaker.

I stared at my best friend, really taking her in. She was one of those friends where you can't remember when or how you met, or when it was settled that you became best friends. She just always *was*. She'd been there for me through everything. Middle school, high school and the fever dream all of that entails. We had even decided to attend the same university—granted, I dropped out after the first semester, but that's beside the point. We've been glued to one another for the better part of half our lives at this point.

She cocked a perfectly sculpted eyebrow, her forehead not even so much as wrinkling while waiting for my answer.

"Yea, no, I'm good." I threw a half smile her way to really drive home that I wasn't into the idea, which only resulted in her rolling her eyes.

"Seriously? Do you want to at least get drinks later tonight?"

"No—" I began, "I have a new book I'm working on and I have a deadline I need to meet, so—"

"Deer, seriously? It's your *birthday*, come on!" I had to stifle a laugh as she tossed her hands in the air, causing the small number of patrons that lingered in the café to glance in our direction. "It's your *golden* birthday!"

I reached for her arms, mouthing an exaggerated 'sorry' to the people side-eyeing us.

"Gracie!" I could feel my cheeks warm at the unwanted attention she was drawing toward us.

She gave me a reluctant look as she lowered her arms.

"You should celebrate," she stated flatly, jutting her bottom lip out.

"I know, I'm just not feeling up to it, maybe next week or something?" I offered.

Gracie perked up. "Wait, you should see if that hot neighbor of yours is home."

She had been over to my apartment a total of one time and already spotted every hot and potentially single man in the whole building. I was in apartment 203, and coincidently my neighbor, Mr. 205, had just been getting home as we were hauling the last of my boxes into my unit.

I rolled my eyes. "Yea, no, I'm not going to knock on some stranger's door and ask if they want to hang out."

"Why? Ugh, just forget about that asshole. He's always been an asshole, always will be! You can't seriously squander away your youth like this! What, are you going to just stay single and die alone?"

Ouch.

"I'm not squandering my youth—who even says that? I just—I don't feel like I'm ready to talk to anyone new. Plus, like I said, I'm not going to knock on a stranger's door! Who even does that?"

"I would! Did you see him? Talk about tall, dark *and* handsome!"

Of course I had seen my neighbor, I had two eyes. I'd made a very strong effort to avoid him. I felt lost enough as it was—I didn't need some pretty boy making things worse for my brain or my heart. A chime emitted from the dark depths of her purse that was slung over the back of the chair behind her.

Please be Vince, please be Vince. I silently prayed.

I watched as she haphazardly reached an arm behind her, rifling blindly through her bag, stealing a quick glance at the message that lit up her phone screen—and then rolling her eyes.

"Ugh, sorry girl. Looks like Vince needs me to swing by the store for snacks for the little gathering tonight." She looked at me apologetically. *Thank God.* "I can grab a cake if you decide—"

"No, no. Thanks, but I'll still pass for tonight." I waved a hand, cutting her off. "Thank you though, really. I appreciate you trying to make my birthday special."

Gracie's eyebrow cocked up again as she shifted to stand.

"I'm serious! No sarcasm! I really do appreciate it." I nudged her foot with mine beneath the table. "*Bestie.*"

Gracie cringed, "Ew, you know I hate when people say that! I'm serious though Deer, Felix *is* a dick and *you* need some dick. Seriously, that neighbor. Or Vince's coworker?" She eyed me and winked.

I gave a soft laugh. Honestly, it was a relief Vince needed her to run around after this, that gave me a perfect excuse to call an end to this little coffee date so I could go home and rot on the couch in solitude. I sure as hell am not going to—what? Waltz over to my neighbor's door and say, 'Hey it's my birthday and my ex-boyfriend is ghosting me, wanna come over Mr. Stranger-I've-Never-Spoken-To?'—Yeah, no.

"Last call for any sad bitches that don't want to be alone on their birthday," Gracie offered.

"I'm good, I promise. It's just a birthday, and you already treated me to a coffee. Besides, I have a hot date tonight with a bottle of wine, a marathon of shitty rom-coms, and my laptop." I shifted in my chair, scooting back just enough to insinuate that I was ready to leave too.

"Okay." She reached behind her and adjusted her purse. "Just, text me if you change your mind or if you want to do something later, alright?"

Chapter 2
Raios

After a year in this city, I had to admit it wasn't much different from home—chaotic, swarming with people... just less *organized*. Speaking of less organized, in the entire year I'd been staying here, this was the first time I'd managed to lock myself out of my apartment. I cracked my neck, pulled my shoulder blades together in a stretch, and sighed. The last-minute holiday I'd decided to take had better be worth it, considering I now faced the option of sleeping outside my door tonight, or knocking on the doors of my neighbors to see if anyone would be open to helping me out.

Come to think of it, that might not be such a bad idea. It would be the perfect excuse to meet the cute redhead who moved in across the hall.

I flipped a metaphorical coin—heads, I took this dumb little error on the chin and slept in the doorway; tails, I take a leap of faith and use this as an opportunity to meet my neighbor.

Deer? Was it?

I was pretty sure that was her name, I remembered when the blond came by to help her move in. That girl's loud mewling grated against my brain with talons I hadn't known existed.

Her voice was so high-pitched and shrill. I shuddered just remembering the caw of her words.

'Deer, oh my god, look at this space! It's too cute! It's perfect!' I grimaced at the memory that flashed through my mind of how that woman's voice breached the paper-thin walls of my apartment that day to punch me right in the ear drum. I'd made it a point to sneak down the hall as unnoticed as possible that day—but I failed miserably.

It was like that blonde's eyes were a heat seeking missile! The moment I stepped foot outside my tiny space; I could feel her hungry gaze raking over my body. I didn't need to look at her to know what that succubus-like woman was thinking. In fact, I made an aggressive point to shun her thoughts from my mind. Instead, I tuned into the somber thoughts of her friend.

Some asshole had wrecked that girl's heart and left it with hardly a pulse. I had never heard or sensed such pain from something that wasn't even close to the brink of death. To be fair though, I had been listening in on her thoughts for a while now and every part of me was convinced I could fix her—that I could be the glue that bound that broken heart of hers back together.

"That settles that," I mumbled to myself and ran my fingers through my hair, hoping the strands cooperated. I had been nervously awaiting this moment.

Today's the day I meet the girl of my nightmares, formally of course.

After all, it was no coincidence I chose Portland to spend my vacation. I had made it a hobby of watching Deer from a distance for quite some time.

Chapter 3
Deer

I kicked my shoes off and left them by the front door, then made a beeline for the kitchen. Now that I was home safe and in the seclusion of my own space, my heart ached and my mind wandered to trying to call Felix again. Was he really not going to send me any type of message or anything to wish me a happy birthday? That's the bare minimum a person could do! I'd think after spending years with someone, they'd at least have the decency to reach out. It's not like he was an ex from years ago; it's only been a few months!

The whole apartment was dark—which was odd because I typically leave at least one of the lights on when I go out in the evening. My mind wandered to my ex for the thousandth time that day and it felt like an iron fist gripped my insides. The feeling was enough to make me want to hurl. Who knew sadness could actually make you feel physically sick!

No matter how hard I tried, day in and day out—I couldn't help but wonder, did he even miss me? The iron fist in my gut seemed to squeeze tighter and it honestly felt as if I'd eaten an entire batch of spoiled oysters. I lazily dragged my hand across the light switch that sat on the wall just outside the kitchen. The ceiling lights flickered on immediately. At least here, in my shabby apartment, I didn't feel the need to put on a brave face and pretend that all was "A-okay in Deer-land!".

I knew he didn't miss me.

Of all the things that relationship taught me, living in solitude was unfortunately one of them. I really didn't mind being home alone so often. Our house—Felix's house—stopped feeling empty not long after he started leaving on work trips. Now, this didn't feel much different—just about 2,000 square feet smaller.

I walked the short distance to the kitchen and swung open the fridge where my wine (and its half-drunk friends) lay dormant, and hopefully perfectly chilled. I snagged one without bothering to look, then checked the door with my hip, closing it with a rattle. My eyes lingered on the pastry I bought myself yesterday for today—sad, I know.

With a sigh, I reached over the island from where I stood near the fridge and snatched the crinkled brown paper bag. It was heavier than I had remembered (I probably didn't need to get the largest cupcake in the case, but dark times called for darker measures). I reached into the bag, already salivating and ready for the sweet release of sugar when my hand brushed something hard and cold.

I cringed, reaching my hand further into the bag as the scratchy paper chewed at the crook of my elbow with its rough edges. *What the hell is that?*

I pulled out a small to-go box, before I cracked it open—to make sure it was safe, of course. The large pale pink frosted cupcake sat perched in gleaming golden foil, with a flower of white icing dolloped on top. I had bought two, but one barely survived the night. Something about sugar turned me into a dessert fiend.

I snorted at the sight, but the decadent smell of confection infiltrated my nostrils, immediately making my mouth begin to water again.

What else did I even buy? I only remembered buying the cupcake.

Shoving my arm back into the bag, I fumbled for the object that gave it all its weight and pulled it out. The bag crinkled loudly, as if in revolt. A delicately wrapped rectangle—heavier than I expected—had been pressed to the bottom. Pulling the wrapped thing from the bag, I took a second to marvel at the wrapping paper. It had a thin, almost satin-y feel, small swans were etched in gold along the gleaming creamy surface. A slow smile crept across my lips, shoulder checking my sadness.

Gracie really went all out, huh? My heart pulled at the gesture; she always made a point to make sure my birthdays were at least slightly decent.

That sneaky bitch must have hidden this in here when she dropped me off yesterday.

Maybe it *wouldn't* be such a bad idea if I watched the meteor shower with her and Vince, and his coworkers. I carefully slid my finger between the folds of the paper, being cautious to not give it any unnecessary tears. I'd for sure be keeping this, call it weird, but I loved little things like this. I already knew I would fold the remnants of the gift wrap and place it in a book later to crease it to my liking before I stow it away alongside other cards and pieces of wrapping paper that I've collected throughout my years of life.

Light refracted off the glossy surface beneath the golden swans, it was a hand mirror. Gingerly setting the paper aside, I examined the present. It was among the most beautiful things I had ever seen. The handle was cold to the touch; ornate designs laced through it and curled around its face. It was perfect. I slid my finger across its defined curves and along the back, feeling the cold bite of porcelain waiting for me on the other side.

Turning it over, a swan floating on dark water decorated the back surface. I had to text Gracie. This was such a beautiful, thoughtful gift. She always knew how much I loved collecting antiques, *ugh*.

Setting the mirror down beside the cupcake, I snatched my phone from my back pocket and quickly sent a text to my best friend.

'OMG, thank you so much for the gift, you sneaky bitch! How did you even manage to sneak that in the bag??? What did I ever do to deserve you?! Ugh, looks like I'll be joining you guys tonight after all—way to guilt me into it with the present. Let me know the address and time, I'll Uber there. Xx'

Chapter 4

Deer

'**H**appy bday D'

My heart sank to my numb feet when I saw Felix's face in a small circle beside his name. I snorted, leaned forward, and rested an elbow on my knee, ready to rapid-fire a slew of bitchy texts. But you know what? He didn't even deserve that. He had *all* day to reach out, and he *just now* bothered to spare me two-seconds for that piss-poor text? It's not like he couldn't see all of my missed calls!

What an unbelievable asshole!

I slammed my phone face down on the coffee table and snatched up the remote, taking my anger out on the small red button protruding from the top, cutting the actors on the screen off mid-sentence. *Fucking asshole.* I don't know what I expected, though. Maybe a '*happy birthday Deer, I'm so sorry for everything, let's get back together!*' would have been nice.

"Insufferable asshat." I murmured, grabbing the wine bottle and cradling it in my arm.

Just as I was about to start my trek to my bed, a knock sounded at the front door and stopped me in my tracks. Another knock sounded, this time louder. My annoyance was already a full-on raging fire, I was half tempted to ignore whoever was out there. My mind stuck on Felix's text—suddenly wishing I had bitched him out, but that meant I would have to actually talk to him and honestly, I know myself well enough to know I would just crumble and pour my pitiful heart out to him (to likely not even get a reply back).

Yet another knock sounded from the door. Somebody better be fucking dying. I lunged for the door, smacked the latch to the left and swung it open.

"What!" I yelled—unintentionally, but not really.

A black-haired man with weird, red eyes jumped back.

"I—uh, is this a bad time?" he asked, running a hand through his hair.

"Yes. Yes, it is a bad fucking time. It's actually the worst time imaginable." I glared. "What do you want?"

He gave a sheepish grin and looked at his feet. "I locked myself out."

"And?" I barked a laugh. "What do you want *me* to do about it? Call the landlord." I moved to close the door on the man's face just as he reached a hand out, stopping it.

I stared at his smooth fingers curling around the edge of my door and glared even harder. Who the hell does this guy think he is?

"*And*, I'm your neighbor in 205—"

"Okay?" I prompted. I was in no mood for any man and I hoped that was painted across my whole face.

His eyes met mine and pink stained his cheeks as he shrugged, shaking his head.

"*And*," he said sarcastically, clearly mocking me. "Can I use your phone to call a locksmith or the landlord—or something? My phone is in there." He jutted his thumb behind him toward his apartment door.

His eyes raked over my face, sweat gleamed off his forehead as if he was either nervous or overheating. It was far from hot in the hallway—was he nervous to talk to me? His eyes were so bizarre, who has red eyes?

Unfortunately, Gracie was right. He was tall, dark, and handsome. To my greatest displeasure, he was the hottest man I'd ever seen. I had purposely paid him no mind when I first saw him in the hallway after moving in. Now, with him just a few feet away, it seemed impossible that I'd managed such a feat.

He blinked silently at me, tossing a dark, wavy lock from his eyes. He let go of his grip on my door and stuffed his hands—hands that looked perfect for a hundred things—deep into the front pockets of his jeans.

"What's up with your eyes?" I snapped out, before I could reel myself in. I squeezed my eyes shut in a long blink and opened them just as his head jerked back at my word vomit, as if he were trying to dodge it.

Smooth one. Mental face palm.

"What?" A flash of a smile seemed to skirt through his features for a moment before disappearing.

"What?" I parroted, hoping—I don't know what I was hoping for exactly. I don't know why I even said that, plus he obviously heard me and now I was the one being the weirdo.

"They're contacts?" he said, his tone rhetorical. "So, can I use your phone for a sec, or should I try a different, more... uh, non-confrontational neighbor who won't question me about the way I look?" He regarded me with an expression that said nothing other than *'WTF is wrong with this woman?'* and dropped his eyes to the bottle of wine I was holding like an infant.

I chewed the inside of my cheek, as he continued eying the half-drunk bottle of wine, which I was *still* cradling like a newborn. His perfectly arched eyebrow raised in wait for my reply. I was being an outright bitch, and I knew it, just taking out my unresolved post-breakup anger on the first man that breathed near me. He clearly just needed a bit of help, and there was no reason for me to *not* help.

I hung my head in solemn embarrassment and self-loathing shame.

"Yeah, yes. I'm sorry, it's been a shit day. Wait here a sec." I grumbled, not able to meet his eyes.

Frantically, I scrambled away and set my precious wine bottle down haphazardly on the tiny entry table. By the time I stepped away toward my phone I heard the heart-breaking sound of my one saving grace shattering against the floor.

Perfect.

I turned to jog back to my neighbor and found him kneeling down picking up the glass shards. He froze as he noticed he had—albeit in a kind gesture sort of way—invited himself inside.

"Sorry," he started. "It felt weird to just stand there and stare at the broken glass. And by the sound of it, you already have enough going on, so—"

"No, no—thanks. You don't have to help. This is kind of you, but seriously..." I held out my phone. "Here."

He glanced at the device, then down at his hands full of glass.

"Right! God, I'm so sorry for being such a shit show. This is embarrassing, let me grab a bag." Once again, I frantically scrambled away toward the kitchen and snagged the first bag I saw.

When I returned there was a pile of glass on the entryway table along with the half-broken bottle. I handed him the phone as he gingerly brushed his wine-stained hands against his jeans. Guilt struck me and I cringed. To be fair, it seemed like this guy was having a decidedly worse day than me. Got locked out of his apartment, asked a neighbor for help (who just so happened to be nothing short of a whole ass bitch in return), then picked glass off the floor in attempt to be nice, just to get wine-stained fingers and jeans—and more than likely a few glass shards lodged in his skin.

He gave me a small nod and a pleasant smile that seemed far too kind, given the situation, and held up a finger to me, signaling he'd be a minute and walked out my door.

Get it together, Deer! I rolled my eyes at myself and began sliding the glass into the bag.

Chapter 5
Deer

Somehow, we ended up on the couch—two wine bottles stolen from my stash of sadness drained, *Supernatural* playing in the background. Apparently, the call to the landlord went straight to voicemail, and no locksmiths were available at eight o'clock at night. Who knew? Gracie would be rolling over in her metaphoric grave if she could see me right now.

"So, are you going to tell me your name or are you just going to sit there and drink all of my wine?" I asked to fill the silence.

He chuckled and took a sip from his glass. "Raios."

"Raios?" I repeated.

"And yours?" he asked, tilting his head.

Those scarlet eyes caressed their way across my face, lingering on my lips for a moment.

"Deer," I stated, my mouth suddenly dry.

"Deer?"

His brows pulled together, and he had no reason to look so hot making such a simple expression.

"Like the animal?"

A nervous laugh bubbled from me and I nodded, taking a sip.

He smiled and I couldn't help but stare, despite his... uhm off-putting contact lens choices, he was hot. Drop dead gorgeous, really.

"And what is it that you do for work, Deer?" He tilted his head the other way as if I were the most interesting thing in the world and flashed me a line of perfectly white teeth.

Oh, so we're really doing this whole small-talk-get-to-know-each other thing.

I wet my lips, suppressing the impulsive urge to recoil. That has always been my least favorite question.

"Oh, I uh, write," I said, avoiding his warm stare.

It always felt so weird saying that out loud, people either thought it was the coolest thing on the planet *or* they thought it was...well, they usually had some condescending shit to say, to put it lightly. Followed by the ever-famous question of *'have you written anything I've heard of?'* to which the answer was usually a sobering no.

"You?" I asked quickly, hoping to turn the attention onto him and away from my life as an aspiring author.

He gazed into the mouth of his cup as if it held the answer to my question.

"Management of sorts. Mainly just watching over people and making sure everyone's pulling their weight." He shrugged. "I'm lined up for a big promotion, I don't necessarily want it, but I'm expected to take it."

"Shitty, condescending boss?"

He took a sip and huffed. "Something like that."

There was a brief pause, as if the conversation had been decapitated by my returned curiosity, and I mentally kicked myself in the ass.

"So, tell me Deer. What made today such a 'shit day' as you say?" he asked, as he lazily ran his fingers through his hair, pinning me with his crimson stare.

I chewed my bottom lip. I didn't want to tell him my boyfriend—well, *ex*-boyfriend—practically ghosted me on my birthday—correction, for the last few years semi-consistently and it was becoming more and more apparent as to how little he had ever actually cared about me. Or, how I had moved here six months ago and still hadn't unpacked. Or that I had a looming self-imposed deadline for my current manuscript, which I wasn't even close to on track to meeting.

Now *that* would be a buzzkill.

Chapter 6
Raios

This poor woman had heartbreak written all over her. I knew the answer to my question before I asked—it was clear by her red rimmed eyes, the way she regarded me with obvious skepticism (and curiosity, which was appreciated).

She was so animated when she spoke, and I couldn't help but find her enthralling. Her hands would work the air as if she were putting on a play and her words were the characters. I decided then and there I would do whatever it took to mend that shattered heart of hers. I'd pick the shards up with my teeth if I had to and take every cut as a blessing, so long as I was the one doing it.

I watched her, keeping my expression as plain as possible as she drew her perfectly pillowy bottom lip between her teeth and mulled over her reply.

A part of me wondered what those plush lips would feel like against mine. What would she taste like? I imagine she'd be sweeter than honey and I'd give anything to taste those lips.

The sound of her voice, so filled with caution, slapped me out of my self-imposed fantasy.

What was I thinking? This girl needed love—someone to show her that she *was* what the universe itself was made of.

That she was all the stars combined into one beautiful, mortal package. And I planned to do exactly that for her.

Chapter 7

Deer

We were both tipsy, and I had to admit—I was having a surprisingly decent time with him. I guess you really shouldn't judge a book by its cover; he was actually nice to talk to. Then again, that could've just been the wine and loneliness talking.

"Uh, well today's my birthday and I don't know, it sounds stupid, but my boyfriend has pretty much ghosted me all day." It felt so embarrassing saying it out loud to a stranger.

Raios' eyebrows knitted together again. "Should I be here right now, I mean like sitting on your couch sharing wine with you?" He looked nervous, which was adorable.

"No!" I all but reached for him but stopped myself. "No, sorry. *Ex*-boyfriend."

I covered my face with my hand. "Forgot the ex-part." I murmured into my glass.

Awkward silence filled the air. *Welp.*

"I mean, like...You don't have anything to worry about. Not that you're doing anything—or, not like *we're* doing anything." I laughed nervously, my heart kicking into an anxious sprint. I was *painfully* aware I was rambling and couldn't stop if my life depended on it.

"I'm sorry. I just mean...this is okay. No boyfriend." *Hello, God? I'm going to need you to put me out of my misery.*

Raios chuckled as he regarded me.

"So, what you're telling me, is you're single." He leaned forward and set his glass down on the coffee table in front of us. "And it's your birthday."

"Something like that." My cheeks were on fire.

I shouldn't have said anything. My jaw clenched as the weight of it settled in—I was starting to feel like I'd ruined the night. Not that I'd been having a stellar one to begin with, not that this was anything *to* ruin. But at the very least, I had started to feel a little less miserable.

Raios mumbled something under his breath that I couldn't quite make out.

"What?" I asked, meeting his eyes. They shined with anger as he shook away whatever the thought was.

"Nothing, I was uh—" He angled his body toward me. His knee pressed lightly against mine and my breath hitched at the contact. "I was just saying, what asshole would *choose* to lose you?"

I blinked at him. *Felix did,* I almost said out loud.

He shifted again, his knee now pressing more firmly into mine, and butterflies stirred in my stomach at the contact. He rested his hand on my knee, palm up.

"Here, come with me." He stood, continuing to offer his hand. "Come on, seriously, I don't bite." He winked.

"Uhm," I began. He wiggled his fingers and the butterflies flew into my chest and seemed to turn into nervous moths.

"Come on, Deer," he coaxed—and I caved. I cautiously slipped my hand into his. His skin was beyond warm, almost hot. It was strange but felt nice, almost comforting.

What was I doing?

He began leading me toward the bed and I pulled back slightly, the butterfly moth party in me died immediately as my stomach plummeted to my feet.

"Oh, no. I'm sorry, I don't know if I was leading you on, but despite Felix being an ass and—and the breakup, I'm, well, I'm not really looking for anything, so—"

Raios looked at me incredulously, as if I just cursed him out and spat on him.

Shit, did he think I was going to sleep with him? Leave it to me to invite a whole ass stranger into my home, thinking this wouldn't turn into some weird shit show.

"What? No, *no*. I'm not trying to hook up with you," he said so quickly I almost felt offended, which made no sense because *I* didn't want to hook up with him first. "Not that you're not beautiful, you are. You're devastating, so, no disrespect to you." His voice made his nervousness evident as he rambled on and tripped over his words—and I believed him.

The weird pang of disappointment when he said he wasn't trying to hook up with me lingered. Not that I was ready to hook up with anyone yet, I didn't think. But a part of me wanted to feel wanted in that way, I guess? I don't know.

He was cute when he was nervous—the way his cheeks flushed pink and his eyes widened slightly. Paired with his dark hair and scarlet irises, he almost looked godlike. But that nervous charm? It was endearing, and for reasons unknown to me, it kind of made me want to wrap my arms around him.

I shook the thoughts from my head. These feelings were so out of left field, I began to wonder if I maybe had a little *too* much wine.

"There's a meteor shower tonight, it should be happening right now...I was thinking we could climb out onto the roof and watch it? I know that sounds dumb, but you deserve *something* nice for your birthday, so I thought maybe—"

"You want to watch the stars with me?" I blurted out.

The corner of his mouth twitched up as he nervously dragged his thumb along my hand, "Yeah... but, we don't have to. Sorry, it was a dumb idea. I feel like I'm just making an already strange situation *stranger*." He backtracked, loosening his grip on my hand. "I can leave now if you want? I feel like I just made things weird."

I huffed. "Leave and go where? It's not like you can even get inside your apartment."

What did he plan to do? Sleep outside his door and wait for the locksmith or the landlord to show up in the morning? He may be a stranger, and I may have been a bitch earlier, but I couldn't just let him sleep in the hall like that—if that's what he was intending to do.

He shrugged as I gripped his hand a little tighter, not wanting to lose his warmth. It was comforting, holding someone's hand. I couldn't remember the last time I had done that. Even when Felix and I first started seeing each other, sure he was fantastic, but he was never really into holding hands. I didn't realize how much I had enjoyed this small thing, until Raios wrapped his around mine.

"No! I'm sorry, it's just been a day. That sounds really nice actually." I gave him the warmest smile I could muster, hoping to put a bandage over the awkward situation.

I laughed and added, "No weirdness here!" As an extra bandage, hoping it sounded less awkward than it felt.

He smiled back as relief washed over his face. He flashed me a line of perfect teeth that resurrected the fallen butterflies in my stomach, causing them to go feral with life.

"Okay then, c'mon."

Chapter 8

Deer

We sat on the sloped roof right outside my bedroom window. It *was* really nice sitting out here, almost nostalgic in a way. Lights streaked the sky and my brain was warm with wine. The butterflies from earlier only grew the longer I was with Raios. Who would have thought sitting on a shabby second floor awning above my downstairs neighbor's window would be so romantic?

He sat hugging his knees to his chest, his night-kissed hair tousled by the breeze. I turned to look at him properly for the first time—and damn, he looked sweet like that. I mentally kicked myself for thinking he was a weirdo earlier. Gracie will *definitely* lose her shit when she hears about this.

"What?" He smiled, but didn't turn to face me, his eyes fixed on the lights in the sky. "I can feel you staring, you know?" His grin widened, causing a hidden dimple to form.

I tensed, "Nothing! I wasn't staring!" My gaze returned to the shooting stars that danced before us.

He chuckled and I could feel embarrassment reddening my cheeks for the hundredth time that evening.

"So, what are you going to wish for?" he asked, turning toward me.

A half-hearted laugh escaped me. I wanted to look at him, but it felt strangely intimate. There was something about sitting on this rooftop with a decidedly hot man—who for whatever damn reason thinks *I'm* beautiful (yeah, that compliment seared itself into my brain). Am I seriously about to wish upon a star with my neighbor on my roof?

Closing my eyes, I sighed. What would I wish for? Love would be nice—real love. Someone who was genuinely devoted to me, cared for me, showed up for me. Shit, at this point, they would need to worship me.

At one point, I had loved my life with Felix. But now, it just felt like I was stuck in a corner of sorts.

I wish for real, wholehearted love. It felt beyond silly to think.

When I opened my eyes, I could feel Raios' gaze on me. I turned to find him resting his cheek on his arm, eyes twinkling while his tipsy, lazy smile remained spread across his face.

"So, did you make a wish?" he asked, and I nodded.

"And?" He prodded.

"*And* nothing, that's against wish-making law. I'm not telling you what I wished for!" I leaned toward him and bumped my shoulder into his gently.

"Did *you* make a wish?" I wondered and he nodded in return.

What would a guy like him even want? He looked like someone who probably had everything and wanted for nothing.

"And what did *you* wish for?" I asked, his gaze was so intense, unwavering.

He shrugged and looked away to the sky. The moonlight gathered around his jaw, making him look nothing short of beautiful.

"Well, per wish making law, I must abstain from saying," he said in a mocking tone. I couldn't help but laugh.

My stomach muscles ached as laughter bubbled from my lips. It had been so long since I had laughed, in fact, I couldn't remember the last time I genuinely laughed like this.

Raios leaned into my laughter, his shoulder pressing into mine. Heat radiated from him, sinking into me where our shoulders touched—he ran so hot, I just wanted to curl up beside him and let him wrap around me like a blanket.

When I looked up, I found him already watching me, his gaze so intense it stole the breath from my throat.

His gaze dropped to my lips, before he forced it back up to my eyes.

"You're devastating," he said softly. "Your laugh is one of the most beautiful sounds I've heard in a lifetime."

I rolled my eyes as I quietly stitched the compliment into my soul.

He looked away, shaking his head, and laughed. The sound melted across my skin like warm honey—but maybe it was just the wine.

"Do you think some people's paths are meant to cross?" He asked suddenly.

The question caught me off guard, even though it seemed a little deep for what I thought was turning into a lightly romantic moment, but I rolled with it.

I mulled the question over for a moment.

"I'm unsure. I guess I think everything happens for a reason and some things have to happen to lead to other things. Like stepping stones, if that makes sense?" The moment the words fell from my lips I knew they were incoherent word vomit.

"Like, if I never met Felix, then I would likely have never become an author." *And let the rambling commence!* "As an example."

Shut up, Deer!

Raios chuckled beside me.

"I get what you're saying, that makes sense." He pressed his shoulder into mine gently.

"And you? Do you think some people are destined to meet, or whatever?"

He nodded as I watched him sip from his glass. His tongue slid between his lips, licking away the excess wine. I couldn't help but watch the way it slipped so smoothly over his perfect lips.

"I do," he said so quietly I wasn't sure if he had said anything at all.

Chapter 9
Deer

It was nearly one in the morning when we crawled back through my window, and I was beyond ready to sleep. I set up the living room couch for Raios, and told him if he woke before me to lock my door behind him.

It felt weird having someone I barely knew sleeping on my couch, let alone a man. Part of me held a strange sense of guilt having a guy sleep over, but it's not like he's sleeping *with* me.

I glanced at the picture of Felix and I, somberly sitting on my nightstand, and felt a twinge of pain. It was a blurry picture of our first date—I couldn't just throw it away.

I sighed and reached for it, placing the picture side down before sauntering to the bathroom. I huffed in frustration the entire five feet to the bathroom. The moment I stepped inside, the weight of the day clinging to my skin suddenly felt suffocating.

I refused to make eye contact with the gray hairs that had begun to sprout from my scalp earlier this year. Once upon a time, this would've been a much longer process—lining my pale blue eyes with the darkest eyeliner I could find, then plastering not one, but two sets of strip lashes on each eye.

Now? Brown mascara and a lip tint was the most I had in me, *maybe* some blush if I was feeling feisty. What was the point? After scrubbing my face damn near raw, I finally fully took in my reflection.

My box-dyed crimson hair had already started fading, silver strands poking through at my hairline, roots growing in. Next time, maybe I'd see an actual hair stylist. It'd only been two weeks with this color, and maybe it was just my own negligent upkeep—or too much faith in a $9 box of dye—but this was *not* it.

I should probably start putting more effort into my appearance. I scoffed at the thought, if Raios thought I was *devastating* like this, I bet his head would roll if he saw me all done up.

No, I scolded myself, grabbing fistfuls of hair and twisting it into a messy bun that flopped on top of my head like a deflated jellyfish. I shrugged off the jeans and sweater I'd been wearing, tossed them into the hamper, and slipped on a big over-sized shirt that might have been Felix's (I know, I know. I really needed to move on).

In nothing but my old favorite bra, socks and underwear—and, of course, the world-famous *ex-boyfriend's old T-shirt*—the air bit at my skin as I pranced to the comfort of the bed. It felt strange being nearly naked with Raios just feet away. Sure, he couldn't see me, but it still felt kind of weird...and also, maybe, kind of hot.

"Goodnight," I said out loud into the darkness of my tiny studio.

There was a soft chuckle and the rustling of blankets. "Goodnight, Deer."

"No, NO!" a man yelled in my dream.

"Stop! NO!" he shouted again, and I stirred beneath my blankets. My eyelids fluttered open, and I wiped the sleep from my eyes. The yells continued, causing me to jolt upright, my heart beginning to pound.

"Please, no!" the voice sobbed.

Did I leave the TV on last night—Oh wait, Raios. *Raios!*

I peeked into the living room and found my guest thrashing under his blanket. Is he having a nightmare? I slid off my bed, dragging my comforter behind me like a cape, and knelt beside the man on my couch, trembling from his night terror.

"Hey," I whispered as I rested a hand on his shoulder. He was burning up—did he have a fever? He seemed to run warm, so it seemed unlikely. Besides, even if he did, there wasn't much I could do; my medicine cabinet was bare.

"Shit," I whispered, my heart starting to calm. Brushing a sweaty strand of hair from his face, I nudged him again, a little harder this time.

"Raios?"

His eyes flew open, pain and fear flooding them as they searched my face.

"It's okay," I whispered. "You were having a nightmare, I think."

His head sank back into the pillow, his eyes falling closed as he slipped back into sleep.

I edged away as quietly as I could, but his hand caught my arm, "Please," he drawled in a sleepy, raspy voice—far hotter than it should have been. "Stay."

Raios lazily scooted himself back against the couch cushions and lifted the corner of the blanket up, a clear invitation, but one I didn't know if I wanted to accept. Was I really about to crawl under the blanket with this stranger who I let stay the night?

It seemed crazy—but then again, I'd already invited a stranger to stay on my couch in a city where I knew only two people. Yeah, it was definitely crazy. I stared at the man, his hair perfectly tousled across his forehead. What's the worst that could happen? Just crawl onto the couch with the hot stranger—sure, why not? Before I could give myself a second chance to skitter back to my bed, I tossed my fluffy comforter on top of Raios and wiggled my way in beside him.

Chapter 10

Raios

Wiggling out from behind the sweet girl I had wrapped in my arms should have been a sin all on its own. Part of me felt embarrassed that I'd woken her up with my night terrors—though, technically, they were hers. Love, was at times, a thankless job, and I'd made a career out of figuring out how to reach Deer over the last few years.

My heart lurched knowing I would have to unwind myself from her, the last batch of hours with her made me feel less lonely for the first time in well—my whole life, honestly.

It sounded creepier than it really was, it wasn't like I had been stalking her. Just more so listening to her thoughts every waking moment I could. I'd be lying if I said it hadn't become a slight obsession, but I couldn't get enough of her. Despite her heartbroken thoughts about the waste of space that broke her, her mind was the most beautiful thing I'd ever had the pleasure of exploring.

I debated whether or not to plant a small kiss on the top of her head. I mean it was right there, and I really wanted to, but I knew that would be off-putting even *if* she was still sound asleep. Besides, I had to get this plan into motion.

It's not like she was going to drag herself to Hell.

I scooted myself out from behind her in probably the most unflattering way imaginable—hooking a leg over the back of the couch and hauling myself up and over the backrest. Safe to say, I was glad no one was around to witness that.

I could smell her on my clothes. The hoodie I'd worn over here now carried a light floral scent—probably her laundry detergent. Either way, I was enamored by the smell and wanted nothing more than to bury my face into it.

Calm down, stop being weird! I scolded myself.

This is no big deal, she seemed to like me well enough. Well, it didn't just seem like it, I could read it plain as day in her mind. She was into me—whether she wanted to admit it or not. Or rather, whether she'd allow herself to admit it. I scoffed and shook my head; I really needed to stop with this business of talking to myself.

I stole a glance over my shoulder, half worried Deer would suddenly wake up, open her door, and catch me—key in lock—at my front door, realizing I'd lied. (But hey, I wouldn't be much of a devil if I didn't lie every now and then, would I?)

My apartment was shamefully bare, with nothing but a mattress on the floor. I didn't care much for human furnishings; they just needed *everything* to be so damn soft *all the time*. It drove me nuts.

Shadows began to swirl around my feet and spill from my palms, it was nearly midday—I needed it to be dark to make this work.

Was it a good plan? No, not really. But it was as good a plan as any.

Whether or not I'd regret what I was about to do...Well, that was debatable.

Chapter 11

Deer

T he next time I woke up, it felt like I had been hit by a bus, killed, revived...and hit by a bus again.

Everything hurt. *Sounds* hurt.

"I am never drinking again," I groaned, rolling my stiff body over.

Why the hell was I on the couch? This was awful. My couch wasn't necessarily uncomfortable, but it was definitely a sitting couch—not a sleeping couch.

I flung my hand out haphazardly and swiped it along the coffee table, praying my phone was somewhere on it and I wouldn't have to move. Moving sounded terrible, I may honestly die if I had to move right now.

My fingers brushed the hard, beat-up plastic cover of my phone. *Bingo!* Thank God. I cracked one eye open—completely unprepared for the assault of sunlight—and peeked at the screen.

Aggressively bright white numbers punched me right in the cornea.

One twenty-three pm.

Fuck.

I swiped my thumb up, revealing several missed texts from Gracie—and even a few missed calls. My best friend and keeper.

I skim-read the most recent message, which had come in about thirty minutes ago.

'Uhm, are you alive? What happened to meeting up last night? Not cool, girl.. If I don't hear from you in the next hour I'm showing up and busting down your door!! Helloooo?!'

Begrudgingly, I sat up, full of regret from the night before, as memories from last night began to resurface.

I really had a stranger stay over, huh?

Insane of me.

Well, at least I didn't get murdered—just the worst hangover of my life. Gracie was going to love this.

"Better just get this over with." I sighed, swallowing back the urge to vomit, and palmed my phone. "Just rip it off like a bandage."

The line rang for a few beats.

"D, are you okay?" Worry clung to Gracie's words with heavy, exaggerated fists. "You didn't answer my texts. Were you seriously still sleeping?"

"Uh, yeah-no, I'm fine. Well, I'm not fine—I have the hangover of a lifetime. So physically, I feel like someone put my brain into a blender, but other than that, I'm fine. I just woke up. So, if you could keep your screeches to a bare minimum that would be appreciated." I put her on speakerphone while I thumbed through the slew of texts, secretly hoping to see one from Felix. "I was watching the meteor shower with Raios, then I went to bed—"

Shit, Raios. I scanned the living room, I woke up alone, on the couch, which was odd, considering I remember falling asleep in my own bed. I kind of remember getting up in the middle of the night to check on him, I think? I don't know, everything is still a wine induced blur.

I glanced toward the door—locked. He must have left at some point, unless—I glanced toward the bathroom, which was open and clearly had no one in it. Bummer. Something about that disappointed me, part of me wanted to see him again this morning.

"Hmph," I huffed.

"Wait, wait, wait. Back up! You watched the meteor shower with *who*?" she squawked, I could hear the sound of her keys jingling and Vince's muffled voice in the background. I wonder if they stayed up all night, it was very likely their night was just now coming to an end.

"Yea." I laughed nervously, "That's the, uh, name of my neighbor. He's uhm, nice? Kind of strange, but nice. He actually slept over... kind of."

The hair on my arms stood on end again, a tingle crawling up the back of my neck. My skin turned hot and prickly, my stomach twisting into a tight knot.

For a second, I thought I might puke—but this wasn't the aftermath of last night's drinking. No, this was that slow, creeping feeling of being watched.

Gracie went silent on the other end, and I finally gave in to the urge to look over my shoulder.

That's it, I'm never drinking again.

"Deer, be so damn for real right now, you seriously hung out with him? Did you guys *do* it?"

"This place has to be haunted, that or the side effects of a night drinking changes drastically as you get older." I groaned and tried to shake the awful feeling. "No, we didn't *do it*, jeez, Gracie. He was locked out of his apartment and knocked on my door, what was I supposed to do? He needed to use my phone and—"

"And so, you let him sleep over, *right.*" She snickered.

"We didn't!" I said quickly. "I was just being nice! I wasn't going to make him sleep out in the hallway."

A thud sounded from the hallway, causing me to yelp, my dehydrated brain throbbing.

"Deer? Are you good? What's going on?"

I turned the volume down a notch on my phone and strained to listen to the hallway. Another loud thud, followed by muffled shouts.

"Do you want me to come over?" she asked, "We could get something greasy to eat, if you want?"

"No," I sighed. "Something's just going on in the hallway, it just caught me off guard." I replied and begrudgingly hoisted myself off the couch to see if I could catch the drama from the peephole in my door.

No one was in the hallway, but a sudden loud slam came from the door directly across from mine, causing me to jump back.

"I think it's coming from my neighbor's apartment," I whispered.

"Why are you whispering? It's not like anyone can hear you in your apartment." She laughed. "Is it coming from Mr. Hottie's apartment?"

"I don't know," I hissed. "Maybe? It sounds like a fight or something, should I knock and see if he's, okay?"

"He's probably banging some chick." Gracie snickered.

"Oh, shut up," I hissed through clenched teeth. Whether or not he was banging some chick—which was none of my business and frankly, I had no reason to care—still opened a small wound next to the heartbreak Felix left behind. "Should I go knock?" I asked again.

I didn't need to ask, I already knew I was going to walk my dehydrated, hungover self over there regardless of Gracie's answer.

Before I knew it, I had my door open and was already making my way to his. I halted in the middle of the hall; I had no idea why I thought this was a good idea. He probably has a girlfriend and maybe they were arguing or something, or maybe they *were* banging. There was definitely shouting.

I sighed, my brain tight and throbbing as if my indecisiveness was amplifying the effects of my hangover. It's not my business and it wasn't like we were friends or anything. It would be weird of me, wouldn't it?

"Uh, I wouldn't?" She quipped, then yelled something to Vince.

Another thud echoed through the thin walls of the apartment building, this time sounding like something hard and large had been thrown or dropped. My heart pounded in my ears, drowning out Gracie's words. The only thing breaking through the haze was the urgent need to check on Raios. The floorboards above groaned, as if someone was walking slowly. The pit that had begun to form in my stomach swelled. What should I do?

I didn't want to call the landlord and say anything, for fear they would just take it as a noise complaint or something and then I would be pegged as the noise police. No thanks. That wasn't the impression I wanted to give. I already felt like I started off on the wrong foot with him last night and didn't want to make it worse with a complaint.

Between the muffled shouts and sounds, it was hard to not wonder if everything was okay in there. From the creak of the floorboards, someone above me was moving down their own hallway—I assumed. Maybe they would call it in, and then I wouldn't have to worry about it or be known as the bitchy, nosy, whining neighbor.

I moved slowly, my bones begging me to crawl back to my apartment.

Making it to his door—against my better judgment and with zero shame—I stretched onto my tiptoes and peered through the peep hole.

Creep of the year.

I held my breath as I pressed into the door, praying no one would walk out of their apartment to find me in full blown weirdo-mode. I was met with complete darkness, which, in hindsight made sense—after all someone looking in from the outside *shouldn't* be able to see into someone's home.

My calves burned, and I respected their cries, lowering my heels back to the floor.

"Stupid," I muttered to myself.

"Did you go back to your apartment?"

"*No,*" I said quietly.

This was so strange, it didn't make sense.

What was I even seeing? Obviously, *nothing,* which made sense to me. But something didn't feel right.

I was fairly positive the fighting sounded like it was coming from his apartment, but then again...I was very hungover. Leave it to me to take the first attention a guy paid me after the breakup and turn it into a full-blown crisis.

He probably had a bad hangover too and was sleeping, someone else in the building must be fighting or something.

I should just call the landlord and let them know about the shouting. It wasn't my place to play police officer or building manager.

"Ugh, okay. Shit—" It sounded like Gracie dropped her phone.

"Ugh, Deer, you should really go back to your apartment. You hardly know the guy. Who cares if he's got whatever drama going on across the hall?" Gracie said, her voice distant and clearly bored. Static briefly overtook the receiver.

"Are you still there?"

"Yes," I groaned. My stomach still felt tight with worry. For some reason I had a nagging feeling that something was wrong behind his door.

"I think I'm going to see if he's okay."

"Ugh, Deer—" Gracie began

"Oh, hush. I'm sure it's nothing, I'm just going to check on him, then I'll get ready, and you can come over. Okay?"

"Keep me on the line in case you walk into a shit show—I want to hear the drama. Oh! And let's go to that new diner that opened up!" She paused. "Actually, FaceTime me! You know how much I love other people's drama!"

"Shut up, I'm not going to FaceTime you!"

Gracie whined on the other line.

I couldn't believe what I was doing. Since when did I care about someone—some complete stranger? Not that I didn't care before, but I'd been so wrapped up in my own misery that I barely noticed anything around me. A one-night-sleepover-stand... was that even a thing?

Stepping back, I took a slow breath in and let it out, hoping to calm the annoying jumble of emotions swirling inside me.

Another crash reverberated through the building and I gasped; this time it was very obvious it had come from inside his apartment. Another thud rang out—this time, it sounded like something heavy had been thrown against the door. I didn't wait. I turned and ran back to my apartment.

Out of breath, my brain feeling like it was caught between two crashing cymbals, I glanced around my kitchen. Thankfully, the open concept made grabbing a knife swift and easy. Better safe than sorry, I didn't know what I was going to be confronted with but I'd be damned if I was caught empty handed. I may be hungover beyond all belief (or naive) but who knows what's going on over there?!

I clutched the handle of the blade so hard my fingernails bit into the flesh of my palm. With my wine fogged brain and best friends annoying comments for fuel, I made my way back over to his apartment.

I slid my feet along the dingy hallway carpet, silently begging them to not contract some kind of disease.

Nerves twisted in my stomach as the reality of how foolish this was sunk in—standing in the middle of the hallway in nothing but an over-sized T-shirt and—

I looked down.

A fucking butter knife.

Crazy neighbor of the year award goes to me!

"Deer?" Gracie chirped. For a moment I'd completely forgotten I was on the phone.

"I'm at his door!" I hissed.

"You're insane! You're actually doing this? I didn't think you were actually serious!" She exclaimed, "Just call the landlord and complain, or the police. Either way, speed it up, because I'm getting hungry."

Standing in front of the door, I slowly crouched down, pulling the phone away from my ear. I quickly slid away the call screen and opened my text thread with Gracie.

'Do not hang up'

Send.

I pressed the buttons on the side of the phone, lowering the volume as much as possible, until Gracie's frantic voice became nothing more than a faint whisper.

Laying the phone just outside the door, I exhaled slowly and rose to my feet.

I knocked on the door, silently praying it was just the hangover making me overthink everything.

Chapter 12

Deer

The door creaked open as my knuckles rapped on the wood—which was weird. Cold air seeped into the hallway, and my skin tightened in response, painfully reminding me I was less than a handful of garments away from being fully naked.

Hopefully no one decided to come down the hallway right now, because I definitely didn't have it in me to explain what I was doing.

I pushed the door open further using the tip of the butter knife. The room was far too dark for the afternoon hour, even if all of the blinds were drawn. It was as if a stray hour of the night sky had snuck in through a window and made itself a home within his four walls.

My breath caught as I stepped further inside, knife still clenched at my side.

"Raios?" I called out, as the crawling feeling of being watched crept over my skin once more.

"Hey, not trying to be weird—just wanted to check on you!" I peeked my head around the door. "I heard some loud noises coming from your apartment and wanted to make sure you're alright?"

I struggled to keep my breathing even, eyes wide as they strained to soak in every trace of light. God, there had to be a light switch around here somewhere. He wouldn't mind if I flicked on a light, right?

I willed my right arm to move, to reach along the wall and search for a switch—but fear kept it bound to my side, stiff and unmoving like a stubborn animal.

Come on, I scolded myself. *You can do this. Just find the switch.* "I'm just going to turn the light on, okay?" I said aloud, more to steady myself than anything else.

The muscle in my shoulder began to cramp from tension. I needed light. Besides, if someone else *was* in here and Raios needed help, there's no way I could help him if I couldn't even see. Realistically, if there *was* some intruder in here, I doubt they would have let me get this far into the room before springing on me. I tried again to glance around the apartment, but still couldn't see a thing—even with the hallway light casting a glow behind me.

I flung my arm out, lunging to the right, my fingers feeling up the wall until they met with the smooth plastic switch. I flicked it up—nothing happened. I teetered the switch between my fingers, willing the light to come to life.

"Hello," a voice so low it seemed to reverberate through my soul, called from the dark expanse of the room.

"Sweet one."

I knew that voice.

I jolted upright, my breath catching in my chest. A mix of relief and confusion swirled within me.

"Raios?" My voice trembled. "This isn't very funny."

An iron fist gripped my racing heart as I took a small step backward. I scanned the darkness in front of me and could've sworn it stared right back. The fine hairs along my arms prickled, my body torn between fight or flight.

"I uh—it sounds like you're okay, so I'll just go!" I tried to call out, but my throat felt like it was closing in on itself and my voice came out as nothing more than a shaky rasp.

Spinning on my heels, I moved toward the door—the sound of it slamming closed stopped me dead. A rush of cold air slid over my skin in heat-starved tendrils. The air began to feel far too thick, and *wrong*.

My grip on the butter knife tightened—I hadn't even realized I'd started trembling. I turned toward the voice, bringing my poor choice of weapon to the front and holding it with both hands.

"And what do you think you'll do with that?" Raios whispered the question into my ear, as if he were right beside me, "Is that a butter knife?"

Damn right it was a butter knife.

His chuckle, I once thought sweeter than honey, was laced with something that wavered on sinister. I swallowed, my throat still tight with fear.

"This isn't funny!" I squealed, whipping my head toward his voice. "Jokes o-over!"

What the fuck, what the fuck, what the ACTUAL fuck!

The feeling of an icy finger swiped down my arm, I fought the urge to recoil and instead slashed at the air. My eyes burned as tears began to form. My poor heart was pounding so hard I was amazed it hadn't broken through my ribs. I spun around to face where I thought the door had to be, the knife slipping from my hands as I searched for the doorknob.

It's too damn dark in here, come the hell on!

I spun around and pressed my back against the wall. The last of my hangover drained away, replaced by fear—well, at least I had that going for me.

Note to future self: say no next time a hot guy locked out of his apartment asks for help.

"Alright, Raios! Ha-ha, very funny little prank," I called out again, my hands still blindly searching the wall for the doorknob.

I don't get it. Why me? Of all the tenants in this building, of course it had to be the hot one—and, of course, he just happened to be a nut job. I froze as Raios' hand suddenly wrapped around my throat, but it didn't tighten. His thumb traced the column of my throat, sending a sickening shiver down my spine.

This time I couldn't help but recoil, shrinking under his touch. If I had any sense left, I'd kick him right in the balls—but fear had me paralyzed.

I could smell him—smoke and lavender filled my nostrils. He was so close. I still couldn't see, but I didn't need to; if I could, I'd claw out his eyeballs.

Unfortunately, all my previous bravery had completely drained out of me. Tears stung the corners of my eyes, a mix of yesterday's pain and the creeping dread that I might die in this apartment flooding through me. His finger crawled up my neck, capturing a tear with his fingertip. A low groan escaped him.

"Divine," he purred.

I stuttered a breath, my knees turning to jelly, threatening to give out on me at any moment.

Something warm and wet slid up my cheek, and the darkness around me seemed to moan in response.

Was that...

Did he just fucking *lick* my tears?

My heart slammed wildly in my chest as my tear-soaked eyes strained against the dark.

Bile rose in the back of my throat, burning like fire.

Maybe if I threw up on him it would buy me enough time to run. Not that I had any idea where I could even run to—if I was fast enough, maybe I could find and lock myself in the bathroom.

"Please," I rasped, my voice a trembling mess. "Just let me go. I'm sorry for intruding."

It was a mistake helping him—and an even bigger mistake thinking it was a good idea to come over here.

Raios hummed, low and pleased.

"But this is what you wished for, sweet one."

My shaking knees finally reached their limit, and I slid down the wall.

"What? Just let me go, alright? I won't call the police. I won't tell anyone about this, or anything." I pleaded.

"No can do."

He sighed, and it began to feel as if the darkness was shrinking around me.

He's going to kill me—the thought cycled through my mind on repeat.

Something akin to a sound of disgust came from Raios.

He pulled me slowly forward, one hand cradling the back of my neck until the sheer, worn fabric that covered my body met a burst of cold air that seemed to writhe around me.

I could hardly breathe. Afraid that if I did... he might—I didn't even know what.

What could possibly be worse than this?

I writhed in his gentle grip, nerves on edge. I wondered if I screamed, would Gracie call for help?

Of course, that's if she hadn't gotten bored and ended the call already.

Which, knowing her, was likely.

I had no idea how long I'd been in Raios' apartment. It felt like hours, but was probably just minutes.

Fuck not being the tattletale neighbor, if I get out of this apartment alive, not only am I moving *far* from here, but I planned to snitch on every damn thing I saw and heard.

My last shred of hope clung to Gracie. My phone was right outside the door. She *had* to hear what was happening.

But if she had...Why wasn't anyone here yet?

I lived right in the dead center of Portland. There was usually a cop around every damned corner.

I should have just listened to her.

Why did I think coming over here was a good idea?

I didn't even know what I thought I could *do*.

Clearly—nothing.

"Your heart is erratic," Raios murmured above me—though his voice seemed to echo from all around. "Like a scared little *deer*."

I squeezed my eyes shut as more tears spilled from them, the darkness no different than when they were open. I shook my head slowly.

"Please Raios," I quietly pleaded.

"Don't think so low of me, little love," he scoffed, "I can see every thought rolling around in that beautiful mind of yours—clear as day. I would never hurt you."

The hardwood floor beneath my feet disappeared, and my eyes shot open—seeing nothing but the darkness. The floor, the one solid thing grounding me, was gone. And with it, my last shred of control. Panic surged through me, full and blinding.

"What the fu—" the sensation of falling overtook me, and I plummeted into the abyss below.

Raios' hand left my throat and slid around my torso, pulling me close as the unending darkness rushed past us in frigid gusts. My hair whipped wildly around my face, and that alone told me—this was real.

This was impossible.

Floors don't just *disappear*.

I was falling.

Fast.

Chapter 13

Deer

"We're almost there," Raios stated, still holding me firmly to his frame. "The entrance is going to be unpleasant, so sorry 'bout that—"

The taste of iron coated the back of my throat, my scream fading into nothing more than a hoarse wail.

Raios slid a calm hand to the back of my head, gently pressing me against his chest as if to comfort me.

My heart threatened to seize and stop at any moment, while my mind struggled to grasp the sensation of falling into nothingness.

A rush of warmth covered my face before slowly engulfing my body, the smell of smoke and lavender filling my nostrils. Before I could even process his words, reality winked out, and I was swallowed whole—mind, body and soul—by darkness.

That's it, this had to be some messed-up, wine-induced dream. Maybe I never even left my apartment. Maybe I was still curled up on the couch, sleeping off my drunken night with a stranger.

I *did* nearly drain that entire bottle of wine.

Yea, that had to be it.

Heat warmed my face. Despite my eyes being closed, I could feel the sun trying to rouse me from my sleep with its bright rays.

I don't think I've ever slept this well in my entire life.

I burrowed my head deeper into the pillow, reveling in its softness, not daring to open my eyes just yet, refusing to give my brain the satisfaction of fully waking up.

Still, I knew I needed to lay off on the wine for a while. Whatever alcohol-induced nightmare that was last night...I'm good on that.

Footsteps echoed somewhere nearby, causing my feeble heart to flutter.

That dream had been the longest, most realistic nightmare I had ever experienced.

The footsteps grew closer and the desperate, sleep-clouded part of my brain echoed *Felix*.

The soft click of the door opening whispered through the room, and before he even cleared his throat, a goofy smile had already spread across my lips.

Giddy with excitement and irrational hope, I rustled free from the sheets and shot upright, all previous anger toward him—as always—washed away.

I popped up from the sheets like a prairie dog—and what greeted me was nothing familiar.

My stomach dropped.

A cold sweat broke out across my skin, as my eyes locked onto a man in a finely tailored navy suit whose hair was slicked back tight against his scalp. His eyes widened a fraction as though *I* had startled *him*.

I pinned him with a glare, feeling like a deer in headlights. He awkwardly stretched his arms out to rest what looked to be a silver platter onto a dresser beside him, the cloche glinting in the light.

Terror began creeping its way into my body and my heart became a jackhammer in my chest as my surroundings sunk in. I glanced down and pulled the covers up to my chest. Holy shit, *holy shit!* Reality closed in around me as my brain caught up to speed. This wasn't a dream.

Leave it to me to think, even for a second, that Felix had magically reappeared in my life. I don't know how my brain even tried to convince me of that. Irritation simmered within me now, shoulder checking the previous terror.

Raios took me.

"Who the hell are you?" I barked.

If looks could kill, I hoped the one I was giving him would knock him right on his prim-and-proper-dressed ass.

The man stared at me for a moment as his body visibly tensed from my tone. His eyes darted around the room, making it abundantly clear he was trying to look anywhere and everywhere other than at me. A flush of pink crept across his cheeks, but he said nothing. Without hesitation, he spun on his heels and bolted for the door.

"Hey!" I yelled after him, but the door had closed behind him with a rushed *thump*.

I took a moment to scan the room once more, trying to recount the last...hour? Few hours? Thick curtains hung in several places, their folds allowing golden slivers of light to slip through the gaps.

Scratch that. Several hours? It had to have been.

A gentle knock sounded from the other side of the door. I stiffened on impulse, but no one tried to enter the room.

Sliding out from beneath the covers, and with a greater effort than I cared to admit—I pulled the flat sheet with me from beneath the hefty comforter.

Cold seeped into my socks as my feet met the floor, the rough stone catching against them.

My face twisted in disgust as I took another step, my socks making an aggravating *schreeeep* across the stone floor. *What shit taste in flooring.*

I draped the sheet around my shoulders as if it were a cloak and sauntered toward the plate the stranger brought.

Whatever hid beneath the petite silver dome smelled deliciously savory. My mouth watered at the thought of the delicious meal concealed beneath.

The closer I got, the stronger the scent. My stomach growled, and I rested a hand against the grumble.

Giving in to temptation, I removed the cloche from the platter.

A warm, buttery steam curled around me.

A beautiful splay of food crowded around the plate that sat beneath the cover. Eggs, bacon, sausage, several slices of different breads slathered with herbed butter. All piled high and begging to be devoured.

I scanned the platter for silverware, but found none and my brows furrowed together. My stomach growled again, pleading with me to dig in the only way it could. But I couldn't allow myself to eat it. What if it was poison?

Knowing my recent string of luck, the delicious butter was probably laced with rat poison.

I mean, sure. Good on the weirdo for trying to offer me a meal. But I'll be damned if I let myself get suckered into an untimely death just because I'm not strong enough to turn my nose up at a good meal.

"Agh!" I groaned.

Deciding I'd be safer if I couldn't see the delicious breakfast, my eyes caught on a small black piece of paper folded and stained with meat grease, crammed beneath the plate.

With careful fingers, I slid the note out and unfolded it.

Welcome! I didn't know what food you liked to eat for breakfast so I had everything I could think of prepared.

I scoffed and crumpled the fine parchment in my fist before tossing it onto the floor.

Glancing warily at the bedroom door, I let out a slow breath. Unease gripped my stomach with a tight fist for a moment, but I forced the feeling aside.

How much worse could things realistically get?

My subconscious begged me to go the coward's way, but my inner 'fuck around and find out' was stronger. What good would it do me to sit in this room like a caged animal?

Where the hell even was I to begin with?

Without giving myself so much as a moment to second guess, I grasped the doorknob and yanked the door open.

I don't know what I expected to see, but it wasn't a dismal stone hall.

The only light provided emitted from suspended lanterns so thickly caked with dust it was a wonder any light shone through at all.

Peering down the hall in both directions, each ended in nothing but darkness. The lanterns barely illuminated more than ten feet around them. *Oh great, more darkness.*

A breeze howled from the dark void to my left, as if coaxing me into going down the opposing side of the hallway.

I took a tentative step over the threshold, stepping directly onto something plush.

My fingers flexed, and my shoulders shot up to my ears.

That *better* not have been a rat.

My stomach sank sickeningly to my soles as I looked down. An all-too-familiar laugh echoed around me, making the whole situation a million times worse.

Frozen in place by the sound, my bad-bitch bravado floated away with the echoing laughter.

For a moment, I forgot that I may have a squished rodent beneath my foot.

I glanced down both ends of the hallway.

Still, no sign of anything, *or* anyone.

But the skin-crawling sensation of being watched slid coldly over me. The voice, the sensation, they both gave me the same unsettling feeling I'd had last night.

"*Dress, please.*" The ominous voice cooed around me.

As if the air itself held an electric current of its own, my hairs slowly began to stand at the command.

"*Now,*" the voice whispered in my ear, as if the keeper of it was nothing more than centimeters away.

Dress? In *what?*

"*Use your head, sweet one,*" The voice murmured, its smooth cadence carrying an unsettling calm. "*Look to your feet.*"

My jaw clenched and unclenched, the unsettling thought creeping in that whoever was speaking had somehow seen my confusion—or worse, read my thoughts.

Hesitantly, I looked down, relieved to find not a rodent beneath my foot, but a folded bundle of plush fabric.

The sheet fell from my body as I quickly grabbed the bundle of fabric, pulling it free from under my foot, and turned back into the room as fast as I could, slamming the door shut behind me.

Chapter 14
Deer

S queezing my eyes shut, I focused on my breath.
In, hold, exhale, hold. Repeat.

I slowly opened my eyes, chancing a glance down at the fabric I held tightly.

Dress, the voice had said.

At least they gave me clothes, I guess. *And* food. I glanced at the platter, but the offering had lost its appeal. Now the thought of eating anything from that plate made me want to vomit.

I can do this. I can get out of here. I needed to believe in myself for once.

Straightening, I shook out the material in my hands. The fabric unraveled as though it was the night sky itself unfurling from my fingertips. A long obsidian gown hung from my grip; the first thing I noticed was that the neckline seemed awfully low cut.

I chewed on the inside of my cheek as I held the dress up to my frame. It seemed to be my size... which was off putting. What an uncomfortable, lucky guess. I sighed out a mix of frustration and defeat. It was either don this random, perfectly sized gown, or move forward and fight my way out of here in nothing but my current outfit.

This is so, beyond, fucked up.

All I wanted was to just spend my birthday wallowing in self-pity. But no, I had to let my hot freak of a neighbor in—and then I had to slink my way over to his apartment to check on him.

I definitely did *not* need to be abducted.

I cringed and used one hand to fling Felix's old T-shirt off of me, before stepping into the dress. To my greatest displeasure, I found it very soft, and comfortable.

The dress hung a few inches above the cold, stone floor. My plain socks looked nothing short of foolish peeking out from beneath the gown.

Could they not have at least given me some shoes?

I searched the room for anything that could be used as a weapon, but the space was beyond bleak. Utterly devoid of anything useful. It hardly looked lived in, or used in general—save for the tousled bedding.

My gaze landed back on the taunting serving platter. I supposed I could use the cloche, or maybe even the tray itself.

Wait! I could use the plate! I stalked toward the tray—yes, the plate could absolutely work!

I snatched it up from the serving tray, tilting it so the breakfast spilled back onto the platter, some slopped onto the floor with an unsavory *plop*.

I crouched, clutching the plate with one fist and slamming it down onto the floor.

Nothing.

I slam the plate again, harder this time. Still nothing.

"Oh, come on!" I yelled, cocking my hand back once more.

A low laugh cascaded around me, making the hairs on the back of my neck raise. I sat completely still, except for my eyes, glancing around the room.

"You're too cute when you're frustrated," a deep voice purred through the space, like some invisible beast stalking its prey.

"Piss off!" I fumed. "What the fuck do you want from me?"

There must be cameras in the room, or maybe some kind of speaker system hidden somewhere.

"But we haven't even begun..."

The sound of the plate clattering on the floor echoed through the room as I stood and let it fall from my hands.

"What do you want from me?" My breath grew shallow with anger.

"Oh, other way around, sweet one. What do you want from me?" The sound of the voice coiled itself around me, like some sort of snake made of ice. *Based on your desires, we both want the same thing. Was that not obvious?*

When I opened my mouth to speak, I felt myself beginning to tremble. I knew if I spoke again, a rush of frustrated tears would gush from my eyes. I couldn't allow that. I refused to be perceived as weak right now.

No. Nobody would want this.

I spoke slowly, "I...I'll do whatever you want, just please let me go home."

As the words left my mouth a soft knock sounded on the bedroom door. I was rooted to the spot, no part of me wanted to open the door to that damned hallway.

I remained tense, staring at the door as another cluster of knocks sounded through the dense wood.

"Can I come in?"

Why even bother asking?

Bile rose to the back of my throat as it occurred to me that my captor could be the one standing on the other side. I glanced down at the plate, lying just inches away from me—it would have to do. I reached down and snatched it up, holding it over my head with both hands.

"Fine," I agreed, the bones of my fingers pressing into the surface of the dish. "Come in, asshole."

If I charge him, maybe I could catch him off guard—

I watched as the door creaked open, waiting for someone to enter, but all that came was murky, dense tendrils of fog.

I swallowed loudly and clutched the plate tighter. I was so sick of these damned games.

The shadows continued to crawl into the room, slithering like starving serpents. I'd never seen fog move in such a manner, never mind that I couldn't recall ever seeing fog *inside* in general, it didn't feel right. The tendrils seemed almost sentient—*that* sure as shit didn't feel right.

I could run through it, but where would I go? Down the equally unsettling hallway?

That seemed like a terrible idea. Instead, I take a shaky step back, away from the oncoming tendrils. The wispy tips of shadows continued to sweep low along the cold stone, as if searching for something. I shake the paranoia from my head.

It's just fog, or shadows...or whatever. Nothing with a brain. It's not going to hurt me. It literally can't hurt me.

The shadows grew closer and all I could come to terms with doing was continuing to slink back, one pitiful step at a time—until I ran into the frame of the bed. My eyes bounced between the shadows that had slowly, but efficiently, flooded the room. Without hesitation, I jumped onto the bed—my mind working overtime to make sense of the situation.

In mere seconds, the floor was engulfed by the writhing shadows, they lapped around the wooden posts of the bed like waves.

My shoulders began to burn as I realized I was still holding the plate above my head.

"You look like a fool." The disembodied voice laughed from all around me, yet again, "What do you plan to do with that plate?"

I whipped my head around trying to find the source of the sound. Whatever game he was playing, I was *well* over it. I bared my teeth and scoffed.

The shadows had made their way on top of the comforter and were now moving toward my trembling legs. A sudden rush of cold rolled in from the hallway, the frigid gust blowing in with enough force to send the stray hairs back away from my face. My skin broke out in goosebumps.

The screaming burn that radiated from my shoulders from holding this plate above my head for so long served as a humbling reminder that I needed to get back to the gym. Who knew a plate could get so heavy?!

The shadows at the edge of the bed began to undulate, just as I lowered my arms. A soft glow no larger than an apple began to form, turning the onyx air gray. Without moving too much,

I peered over the edge of the bed. My stomach tightened while I watched the shape expand.

What in the fucking hell?

Gray quickly transitioned to white. The first thing to break the surface of the hazy mix was two pointy...spikes? My eyebrows pulled together as the whatever-it-was continued to rise from the fog.

What had started out as fine points quickly revealed themselves to be stout horns. Horns that were nestled atop a dark-haired scalp, which breached the fog next.

Pins and needles shot across my face, a sudden reminder that I had barely sucked in a single breath while watching. I had been too enthralled by this living nightmare to register my lungs were screaming for oxygen.

Unblinking eyes emerged next, irises as red as freshly spilled blood—looking right at me. A mouth followed, curled in a hungry smirk, as finally, the body emerged.

I'd recognize that hot, chiseled face anywhere.

"No fucking way," I whispered.

"You swear far too much for such a devastatingly beautiful thing," he said as his smile grew.

Spots began to dance across my vision, my periphery slowly disappearing.

"Raios?" My words were beyond weak, strangled by fear.

"Hi, Deer." His hungry smile turned warm. "Breathe, love."

My fight or flight instinct malfunctioned and left me frozen as I tried to grapple with reality. My mouth was beyond dry, my tongue sticky. For a breath, we just stared at each other in silence.

He dipped a shallow bow and extended a hand out to me, his porcelain palm facing up. His muscles flexed as he reached toward me slowly and raised his head slightly, level to mine. He frowned slightly and began to withdraw his hand when it became clear I had no intention of taking it. He looked as if the rejection had wounded him, his disappointment was evident.

The corner of his mouth twitched downward as he then scanned the room, "You didn't eat," he said, all too casually.

I offered only a blink in response, unsure what to say, if anything at all.

"You really should have eaten." He exhaled. "We killed nearly two bottles of wine last night. You need food."

His words filtered in through one ear and out the other. My focus was still stuck on his face, and the two finely pointed horns that seemed to protrude from his temples. I knew my mouth was opening and closing like a goldfish. I probably looked beyond foolish. I didn't care.

He sighed, stepping toward the bed with soundless grace. "Very well."

"What are you?" I asked as I recoiled from him.

An all too sweet smile unfurled across his lips as he gestured to his horns.

"You tell me."

Chapter 15

Raios

Well, none of that went as planned.

I felt bad about all of it, I could have done away with the creepy entrance and the shadow show, but I selfishly wanted to make a spectacle out of it. I wasn't entirely sure how to reveal myself to her, ripping off the bandage seemed like the easiest thing at the time.

While she gaped at me, I could see her fear, her confusion, as well as the exhaustion roiling behind her eyes, which made me feel even more guilty. As I watched her, I saw the color drain from her face, quickly... a little too quickly.

Fuck, was she about to—I watched as she collapsed to the bed.

I stood, stunned, at the foot of the bed. I had expected her to freak out, but faint?

I sighed and hung my head. If only I had googled, "*how to tell the girl you like that you're a devil and have her understand you mean her no harm and actually like her and want her to know that she's*"—

"Do you want us to do something?" A voice chirped.

I glanced over my left shoulder to find Cam and Mal walking through the door, and sighed.

They both eyed the heap of girl on the bed and Mal smirked.

"Smooth." Was all he said.

I groaned.

"Get one of the elixirs, that should wake her up," I mumbled, trying to shove my embarrassment elsewhere.

The elixir was basically a smelling salt of sorts, actually it was closer to a glucose tablet or whatever those hockey-puck-like things are that people sometimes had to eat up top. Either way, it was made from a mineral down here and was so sickly sweet most dwellers here used it to jump start their day. Or, I supposed in this case, to wake someone up.

Chapter 16

Deer

"**I**s she alright?" a voice whispered, uncertainty lacing their words.

"Yes, of course she is," huffed a second voice, though it sounded more like an attempt at reassurance than certainty. A sharp jab in my side forced a groan from me.

"Well, what did you do that for?" The first voice questioned again, wavering between concern and accusation.

"I didn't do anything! I was just making sure she wasn't *actually* dead. It doesn't seem like she handled his entrance well," the second voice exclaimed, defensiveness creeping in.

"You ought to be more careful, Mal! Here, give her the elixir."

A third voice laughed, seemingly amused by the situation, a stark contrast to the tension between the other two.

There was a scoff, followed by the sound of glass clinking against glass, before something cold pressed against my lips.

My eyes flew open as shock flooded through me.

Had I seriously fainted from fear? Fight, flight, and then there was me—fainting. I flung my arms out, knocking away whatever they were trying to make me drink. The light was bright and blinding, as if someone opened all the curtains. Three blurry shapes hovered in my vision.

80

The third voice laughed, then there was a shift in weight around me followed by a huff and some incoherent mumbling.

"Morning," the voice hummed, a mix of amusement and curiosity played on their tongue. "That wasn't exactly how I wanted to make you black out."

My eyes finally focused on the people before me. Three men. Well, two men and one horned, whatever the hell—goat man? Monster?

Raios.

"Devil," Raios said, as if reading my mind. "Though, goat man does have a nice ring to it."

Okay, maybe he *can* read my mind. Great, so my hot neighbor not only turned out to be bat-shit crazy but is also a mind reading goat man devil.

His lips curled up into a kind smile, as I finally met his eyes. Something about it—as unsettling as it all was—was enticing. He leaned back casually onto his elbows, giving me a chance to notice his shirtless state. Of course he would be shirtless, because why *would* he be wearing a shirt. That would just make too much sense!

Try as I might, I couldn't stop my gaze from straying to his exposed torso. What kind of woman would I be if I didn't? It's right there, demanding my attention—perfectly sculpted muscle and all.

Despite the terror of quite literally all of this, he's not *not* hot and I'm not above acknowledging it.

Snap out of it, Deer!

One, he's clearly mentally unwell, considering he abducted me and literally dragged me to—wherever the hell this place is. And two...well, yeah, he abducted me. But I'd be lying if I said that from the brief five seconds (I counted) I looked at him, he wasn't heartbreakingly gorgeous—in a dangerous 'get too close and I might spear you in the heart with a horn' kind of way.

Something about seeing him like this did things to me, *unwanted* things. He looked good last night—sure, but there was just something about him, now, that was different—and no, it was not because he suddenly had horns. Those horns—they had to be fake, same with the red eyes—no one had red eyes. He even admitted they were contacts last night. The horns must be prosthetics. Yep, that explanation makes the most sense. So, why did doubt still linger and gnaw at the edges of my rationality?

He shifted on his elbows and jerked his chin slightly, as if signaling to someone. Two men in twinned tailored suits edged closer to where we sat on the bed.

"Mal and Cam will prepare and inform you of this evening's plans," Raios said, his gaze so intense it was as if he was looking into the making of my being.

"N-no thanks," I said, as if his statement were an offer. "I'd like to go home actually. This has been freaky and fun, best birthday ever. Woo-hoo and all, but I think I should get going."

I didn't know if there were five stages of shock, like there was with grief. But, if there was, I think I was entering the "bargaining" phase.

I made a move to slide off the bed, until shadows began to form beneath him, slowly encapsulating him in silk obsidian until he was nothing more than a shadow of himself. The smoke lingered for a few breaths before one of the suited men came to take his spot on the bed, waving the smoke away with a hand, while the other one followed suit and sat down, mirroring the same movements.

Stunned, I sat there, half off the bed, blinking before glancing toward the two strangers I was left with. I wondered if they had seen the same thing.

Glancing between them, I realized they were identical in every manner of the definition. I huffed, *twins*.

"What—" I began to ask sharply, noticing their stares.

"Camroth," the one on the left stated while offering a surprisingly charming smile.

"Mal," the one on the right said, giving a small nod and a wink.

"What—" I began again, this time a bit louder, only to be cut off.

"You are set to dine with Raios in the dining hall in precisely fifty-seven minutes and twenty-six seconds." They spoke in unison.

Well, that's specific.

"Yeah, no. I'm not dining with him; I need to go home. That horned asshole—you can tell him to take one of those horns and shove it right up his—"

Mal and Cam looked at one another, eyes flicking back and forth as if they were in some sort of silent conversation.

"Raios," Mal began.

"The prince—" Cam continued.

Prince?

"He'll be awaiting you; it is in your best interest that we get you prepared," Mal claimed.

"Tonight's a big deal for him, for both of you really. He wants to make this a special night," they said in unison.

"We now have fifty-four minutes and thirty-nine seconds to make sure you are ready," Cam announced, rising from the bed with a determined stride toward where I had cornered myself.

I pressed myself harder against the headboard, wishing I could somehow meld with the wood and anchor myself there.

"I'm not doing anything with you two. And, I am not going to *dine* with anyone," I growled, riding a humble wave of determination and defiance. "Let. Me. Leave."

"Oh, I don't think you want that." They intoned together. Their odd synchronization sent a shiver down my spine. It was eerie, yes. Honestly, it was more so, the sound of their voices together grated against my brain like nails along a chalkboard.

I shot a glare at the two men, tension coiling within me like a spring ready to snap. Just one more tandem utterance and I felt I might reach out and tear the tongues straight from their mouths.

Much to my *not* surprise, the more I looked at them the more it registered that, of course they too were hot—in a weird 'hey this is fucked up' kind of way. Two perfect mirror images of one another, both in tailored navy suits, both with the same slicked back black hair that framed amber eyes. They honestly looked a little bit like Raios.

"You can't tell me what I want. How would you two assholes know?" I snarled, my fingers knotting the sheets. My palms were slick with sweat. "I *want* to go home. I *don't* want to be here, wherever *here* is."

"We now have forty-nine minutes and three seconds," they said plainly, in maddening unison.

Aaaand *pop!* There went my sanity.

84

"Oh my God! Will you two stop that?" The words erupted from me as I pressed my fists deep into the mattress. "Stop with the ominous count down!"

Cam and Mal looked between one another, their eyes flicking back and forth, before nodding curtly. Their movements were swift and caught me off guard as they hoisted me up off the bed like a toddler throwing a temper-tantrum. They each had one hand underneath an armpit and the other clasped tightly around my forearm.

"Hey!" I wailed and thrashed wildly in their grip—legs flailing in a furious attempt to land a hit. Unfortunately, my efforts were utterly futile against their iron grip as they stalked to the door.

Chapter 17
Deer

I was beyond drained, both mentally and physically. The air around me grew heavier as I was unceremoniously dragged out of the room—my struggles proving to be as effective as a feeble mosquito against iron. I gave up after the first thirty feet down this seemingly never-ending hall.

Wherever they were taking me, it felt like it was taking forever to get there. I stole a glance at my wardens, the dim lighting of the hallway made them appear as nothing more than shadowy figures—though, it also carved sexy shadows along their jaws. I rolled my eyes and tried to catch a glimpse of something, anything, that could give me a clue as to where I might be or where I was being taken. The hallway was empty and cold—nothing but dust covered lanterns and cobwebs lined its stone walls.

The longer we walked, the colder the air seemed to grow, the temperature dropping with each step. My teeth had begun to chatter uncontrollably and I could see my breath in front of me—puffs of white hung in front of my eyes, clouding my vision.

We turned a corner and finally came to a stop in front of a large, ornately carved wooden door. Oh, *thank God!*

My armpits had become beyond sore from their hold on me. I hoped this meant they'd, at the very least, release their grip on my underarms.

Cam knocked a few times; the raps were a specific beat, almost like Morse code. After a moment, the door groaned open and a rush of warm light spilled into the hallway as a blast of heat hit me. The sudden change in temperature burned my skin and sent a current of tingles throughout my body. I squinted against the hot air as the door continued to open, revealing a grand room filled with ornate furniture and rich tapestries—worlds better than the one I had been in.

This room had *nap* written all over it—if it weren't for the circumstances, of course.

A hearty fireplace, encased in black marble, commanded the back wall. What I would give to curl up in front of it on the lush fur rug spread out at its base.

"Thirty minutes and twelve seconds," the twins stated.

My head dropped back as I prepared to groan, but as I did, they released their hold on me. My head snapped back and my eyes flicked between them, as my legs urged me to turn and run.

"This way please," Cam spoke softly and brushed a hand along my arm, coaxing me to follow them further into the room.

I took a tentative step forward—the heat was seductive...it *was* a lot warmer in there.

"I wouldn't advise you to go back into the hallway alone," Mal said from somewhere, seeming to have disappeared within the room.

"And, why's that?" I asked, half curious and half not giving a shit. I glanced over my shoulder towards the dismal, dark, frigid hall.

"Try it," Cam said dryly.

He looked at me with an expression so blank it had apprehension swarming in the pit of my stomach and I froze at the offer. There was a pause between us—me, unsure of what to do, and him...well, I figured his patience was starting to wear thin.

"Twenty—" Mal called as Cam gracefully lunged toward me.

His palm connected with my shoulder as he shoved me backward and before I could yelp, my feet tripped over one another. My back fell through where the door should have been. A delayed scream burst from me as I flung my arms behind me to catch my fall, only to find that I continued to fall. There was a brief rush of frigid air over my skin, my vision tunneled and warped, everything elongated as the motion continued. Then—just as suddenly as it began—it stopped.

I was in front of Cam on my hands and knees, panting.

"—minutes and sixteen seconds," Mal finished.

"What was—" My head spun, and I gagged, dizzy. "*That?*"

Cam's hands found my armpits again, and hauled me to my feet, bringing us nearly chest to chest. I breathed heavily through my nose, my stomach churning like it was caught in a violent spin cycle. *Always with the damned armpits.*

Mal appeared before us. "We won't have enough time."

He now wore a crimson crushed velvet suit—which would look hideous on most men, but somehow on him was captivating. Noticing my stare, the corner of his mouth twitched up and I quickly averted my eyes and made a feeble attempt to wiggle away from Cam.

"Give her to me, I'll start." Mal reached a hand towards me, his palm open and oddly inviting. "Ready yourself, Cam."

Mal's hand flexed toward me, eagerly awaiting mine. Half begrudgingly, half nauseated, a small part of me wondered how his hand would feel around mine. So, I slid my hand into his as Cam walked away from us. His skin was warm and soft, not quite as warm as Raios' but warmer than normal. There was something oddly calming about the way he absentmindedly ran his thumb over the top of my hand. His touch melted away the nauseated feeling that had taken place within me. My heart fluttered at the way he gently held my hand in his—the reaction my body had to his touch felt so out of left field.

I let him lead me toward a lavish canopy bed adorned with rich fabrics and intricate carvings.

"Sit," he commanded. "Please."

He let go of my hand and I sat at the edge of the bed—not exactly liking where this could be going. Sure, he was hot. Strange, for sure, but hot. Something about Mal was intoxicating and calming.

I kept my eyes on the floor as he stood before me, crossing his arms and letting out a sigh.

"We have fifteen minutes, zero seconds," he whispered under his breath.

"Okay, seriously? What's with the creepy countdown?" I could feel his eyes on me as he stepped toward me in silence. I instinctively pulled away.

From the corner of my eye, I watched his hand rise to my face, a finger hooking gently under my chin to tilt it upward.

I avoided his smoldering amber gaze, staring instead at the fireplace across the room. His other hand came up, fingers brushing softly through my hair.

I braced myself for the sharp snap of knots being forced apart, but instead, I was pleasantly surprised by the sensation. This was all so confusing. My mind was a hornet's nest of contradicting feelings and thoughts.

"Hmm," he hummed.

From my periphery, I watched as he lifted his thumb to his lips for a breath before bringing it to my face. My eyes snapped to his, brows pulling together and widening as he brushed his thumb over my lips, something warm coating them.

"What was tha—" I began against the brush of his finger.

"This is going to have to do," Mal said softly and sighed, releasing my chin just as Cam appeared behind him in a matching suit.

I ran the tip of my tongue along my bottom lip; sweet iron coated my taste buds. Instantly my stomach clenched.

"Did you...is that your blood on my lips?" I yelped, reaching up to wipe my mouth with the back of my hand.

"He's going to be annoyed," Cam sighed, regarding me.

"Very," Mal said, his voice low and serious. The twins' hands gripped my shoulders firmly.

"Best of luck," they intoned in perfect unison. Without warning, the world around me plunged into darkness.

Chapter 18

Raios

I stood staring—my face colored in shock, at my parents. Panic swelled in my gut, as I asked, "why are you guys here?"

This wasn't ideal, in fact, this was bordering on disaster. I had planned a nice dinner for Deer, a first date of sorts—hoping it would be a smooth transition which would present the opportunity to explain myself. Having my parents stop by was far from what I had wanted for tonight.

My mother scoffed and my father sighed into his hands.

"What, no hello? One would think you'd be delighted to see us!" My mother sneered.

"Yea, so great. I love your little visits," I mumbled.

"Sorry, come again?" her tone was sickly sweet, as she cocked her head in my direction.

"I said, it is *so great* to see you. I *love* when you visit." I did my best to force a smile, but knew it showed as a grimace at best.

This is awful—beyond awful. Deer's first night in Hell would *actually* be hell with my mother here.

"What is it, son? From the look on your face, you'd think we just showed up and told you our eternal damnation had been lifted, and we're moving to heaven." She barked a laugh.

"I have a guest," I said firmly.

"A guest?" Mother mused while looking toward my father, whose head remained resting in his hands. He may be immortal, but she's aged him.

"Yes, an important guest. We are set to dine here and she will be arriving shortly, so I *need you to leave*," I urged.

Fuck.

My mother cackled wildly as her eyes widened in surprise. "*She*? Did you hear that Stan, our son has a woman coming to dine with him! And to think, all this time I was convinced that I would have to be the one to find you a suitor to rule with you in your father's place!"

I couldn't stand how she called Father *Stan*. Honestly, to my bemusement I couldn't believe he allowed her do so. She caught my glower and leaned forward, propping her chin on a fist.

"Oh, relax Rai. I'm just surprised is all! Your father was already ruling Hell at your age, so forgive me for thinking this day would never come."

I winced. "Don't call me that. And Father only ruled so young because he had the misfortune of being arranged to have *you* as his mate, Mother. Forgive me for wanting to enjoy who I spend my eternity with."

She rolled her eyes and waved me off.

Chapter 19

Deer

"Is her respect lost on us?" An angry voice boomed from all around me.

The air was thick with the scent of sulfur and smoke. Screams and howls erupted all around me as I speared through darkness. My mind swam—each sound was like a punch straight to the brain. I squinted, seeing nothing but hazy shades of red and black.

"What?" I whispered, dazed, as I struggled to rouse my brain into working.

It felt like I had been vacuumed out of my body and slammed back in, all wrong and jarring.

"You brought that? Surely, this is a farce, Raios." A voice rang out, baffled and sharp.

"A mortal? What in the inferno is this? This is a joke. Please, Son—tell me you cannot be serious."

"Direly, Mother," a low gravelly voice I recognized to be Raios' replied.

There was an eardrum puncturing wail, followed by the sound of glass shattering. I flinched at the noise as my vision finally came into focus—and boy, did I really wish it hadn't.

"She can't even bother to look at us, let alone greet us! You chose *this* vain thing?" A glass shattered.

"Seph, she's adjusting. Mortals aren't used to the way we travel." These words were so softly spoken, almost timid.

I stood in a cavernous dining hall of sorts, surrounded by black stone covered in carvings of writhing bodies, their forms contorting in ways which defied human anatomy. Above me, a chandelier made of obsidian and blackened bones cast an eerie glow, illuminating the long table sitting in the center of the room piled high with food and three sets of expectant eyes.

I winced as warm skin brushed against my chest, catching me off guard—then suddenly, it felt like Lucifer himself had unleashed hellfire on me. My chest burned, raw and searing.

Panicked, I glanced to either side, expecting to see Cam and Mal...but I stood completely alone. "There. They're bonded. Now, can we get on with this meal?"

I tracked the voice with my eyes. A man who looked no older than forty sat at the head of the table, exhaustion hanging from his eyes in the form of deep purple crescents.

A low laugh rumbled through the air.

"Fantastic. *Faaaaantastic.*" The woman who sat to the man's left wretched.

I knew I must've looked completely lost, and the longer I stood there, the more the woman's expression twisted with irritation. I couldn't help it, though—Raios, now hornless, walked toward me. His blood-red eyes sparkled with joy, and that familiar, pleasant smile spread across his face.

"You're late," he breathed through his teeth.

I squinted at his forehead; he looked so normal now.

"I don't need them all the time, I can choose to have them show or not," he stated as if reading my thought. "Now, please.

Join us. I know for a fact you have not eaten yet, and well—my parents are apparently waiting to meet you."

Shock seemed to have fully taken over at this point. I stood there, dumbfounded by how casually he spoke, as if this were all normal.

"Please?" There was a particular begging tone to how he spoke, as the soft heat of his palm enveloped my hand.

"I don't understand," I began.

"Well, you were to dine with just me—as I said earlier. To be fair, I wasn't expecting my parents to show up. They're not accustomed to seeing mortals—just so you know—so please, treat them with grace." There was a hint of sarcasm in his voice, as if he found humor in the situation.

Grace, the word hit a chord in me.

Gracie!

I tried to recall when I had spoken with her, but the more I pushed my mind to find the memory, the murkier and more distant the thoughts became.

Raios snickered beside me—at my expense, I'd wager. I fought against the attraction buzzing through me from the sound of his laughter. His head tilted back as the sound poured out of him, infusing the air with the intoxicating rhythm of humor. I watched, surprised rather than distraught by the sudden outburst.

"Come—" he wrapped his hand tighter around mine. "I'll do all the talking, don't worry, my little nightmare."

He had been throwing so many pet names at me—it irked me more than it unsettled me, but I'd be lying if I said they didn't make me feel a certain way. There was a shuffle of feet and a symphony of whispers. I rolled my eyes but followed him to the table where his parents sat.

"My Queen," Raios said with a smirk as he gave a low, exaggerated bow and pulled a hefty oak chair out for me. The wood scraped against the stone floor awkwardly in the silence.

I glanced at his parents, feeling strange and floored by the audacity of the whole scenario. I could go about this in one of two ways; play along and maybe he'd somehow be down to let me go, or pick up the fork that gleamed in front of me and start jabbing. I could see Raios biting the inside of his cheek, amusement filling his eyes as he watched me hesitate to sit.

It would be three versus one, I sighed. Might as well play along and play it as safe as possible.

Sliding into the chair I gave a small nod, meeting his eyes as he stood above me while pushing my chair in. His eyes were locked on my chest, and suddenly I became aware of the sting that lingered there. I brushed my fingers over that sensitive, mysterious spot on and winced. The skin felt slightly raised—yet another thing to add to my ever-growing *"figure it out later"* list.

"Right, so, let's get this over with. I don't have any intentions on acquainting myself with mortals." His mother sneered at me as I forced myself to calm down and take the situation second by second.

I plastered my sweetest smile on my face as her eyes overflowed with disgust. Raios slid into the chair beside mine, moving it so his armrest was practically touching mine. Keeping my eyes on his mother, I reached across the wood separating us and placed my hand on his thigh, before tracing circles along the black velvet encasing his leg. He tensed beneath my touch, surely not anticipating the change in my demeanor.

If she was going to play bitch, then let the games begin.

"We will be leaving after this dismal meal." She eyed my movements and scoffed, looking at the array of food as if they were piles of shit. "Your father has a meeting in the north with your uncle. If you are serious—which I certainly hope you are not—about this..." Her eyes were on me again. "*Hound,* then we will leave it up to you to commence the ritual."

I coughed out a laugh and tilted my head at Raios, whose eyes met mine with an amused expression—like he was up for playing this game of chicken with his mother. He raised an eyebrow at me as I kept stroking his thigh, feeling a bit braver fueled by spite.

"Mother dear," Raios said, his tone dripping with venom, "you're the only hound present here, as you so *graciously* pointed out. What did Father marry you for, again? The noble task of bearing heirs?"

His eyes left mine and locked onto hers, lips curling into a cruel smile.

"And yet, after millennia, you've given him just one. What a disappointing *hound* you turned out to be."

Wood grated sharply against stone as she shot up from her seat, his words hitting their mark.

"You despicable, miserable, waste of seed." She bristled and I had to fight the smile that was threatening to creep across my lips.

"What a disappointing thing for a mother to say to the only heir she could provide the Underworld. You're dismissed,

Mother." He waved a hand lazily in front of him, as if swatting at a gnat.

This *was* entertaining.

See, if Raios had led with this, I probably would have been a little less pissed off and freaked out.

I snuck a glance at his father, who looked like the bickering was draining the life out of him with every word flung across the table. He just sat there, silently rubbing his palms along his forehead—I couldn't help but wonder if he had horns too.

"Now, my sweet one. Would you prefer to be on top—I'd love to watch you writhe around on my cock, while you curse my name in front of all the Underworlders. Or, perhaps you'd like to be bent over? So you can watch as the crowd pleasures themselves to you being fucked," Raios purred.

I whipped my head toward him so fast I nearly smacked my head against the back of the chair. "Huh?" I gaped, my heart skipping from his outlandish words.

My hand stalled on his thigh. Plates and glass shattered somewhere across the table, but I couldn't even look, I was too baffled by what he'd just asked me.

This sweet—debatably twisted, and undeniably hotter than hellfire—man just asked *what*? What shocked me even more was the fact that he asked me something like that right in front of his parents.

Raios' eyes were intense with an emotion I couldn't quite pinpoint, but definitely was beginning to feel suspiciously interested in exploring. The butterflies I felt the first time we interacted appeared in my stomach, attraction overriding rationality. Wood hit the floor somewhere within the room with a loud crash, startling my attention away from the heated moment. I turned to look toward the sound and found that his parents had vanished. I stared at their empty chairs and swiveled my head around.

"Well done," Raios praised me.

"Don't worry, they're gone and likely will not return for a long time," he assured me. "I'm sorry you had to meet them. I had no intention of our first date going like this, honest."

My eyes widened. "First date?" I spun toward him.

"Yes, first date," he said with a sheepish grin. "The first of many—I'm hoping for a few millennia's worth."

"What?" I asked incredulously.

He nodded. "I know you heard me correctly, Deer. I can sense it in your mind. What do you say? Would you care to date a devil like me?"

I stared at him, completely baffled.

This was a *date*? Our *first* date? Says who? I didn't agree to go on a date—especially one like this! This felt more like a nightmare than a date. This man was bat shit crazy.

His smile faltered, and for a moment, I caught a flash of sadness in his eyes.

"And, if I say no?" I ventured.

"Well, this was *your* wish. I'm fulfilling it. It's a devil's duty to grant the wishes of the desperate. Up north? They get the prayers and hopes of the good. But down here...down here, we get the pleas, the bargains, the desperate exchanges. You can deny me, deny *this*. But whether you admit it or not, this *is* what you wished for."

I was pretty positive that I hadn't wished for a *devil*, let alone to be abducted by one.

He *was* drop dead gorgeous though, I'd give him that. Then there was the fact that when he looked at me it felt like he was looking at every fiber of my being, seeing me for me. Which I'm not sure any man had done before.

I couldn't possibly date a devil though, right? That would just be...

"What happens if I deny you? Do I get to go home?"

He shrugged. "I don't know. I've never been denied before, but I'd assume—based on my father's stories—you'd end up trapped here in some way, shape, or form."

"And where is 'here'?" I asked, slowly.

"Deer," he drew out my name as if savoring every letter.

I stared at him, everything in me stilling.

"Where is here?" I demanded, my voice taking on a small shake.

"Hell," He replied flatly.

I remained silent for a few moments, giving him the silence to add in the real answer—but, when he said nothing more, I realized he may be serious.

"I *am* serious," he said quietly and I cringed at the reply.

"Prove it."

He looked at me in surprise. "Prove it? How?"

I shrugged.

His eyes never left mine as his horns emerged from his head, smoke pluming from them in small puffs. The look he gave me was enough to let me know he knew I needed more than just that, and he sighed.

He reluctantly raised his hand and made a strange wafting gesture, turning the room black for a moment. Shadowy forms suddenly began writhing around us. The shapes cackled and yowled, their wispy fingers reaching for me, causing me to jump up from my chair. Raios had found my hand, and pulled me back down into my seat.

The room instantly went back to normal and I hauled in a deep breath. I could feel that all of the color had drained from my face.

"So..." he said slowly, "what do you say?"

I sat tensely in my seat, shaking with fear at what I had just seen. He seemed serious, even if he wasn't there was no way for me to believe otherwise.

"Do I need to sift through all those thoughts or will you put me out of my misery and just tell me?"

"Okay," I whispered.

"Okay?"

He reached toward my face, his warm palm cradling my cheek as he began to stroke it softly. Similarly to Mal's touch, the rigid feeling of unease began to melt away.

"You will never see anything like that again, I can promise you that, Deer. I'm sorry. I know that scared you, but you asked me to prove it. That place you just saw was the Hall of the Damned—no place that will ever concern you, nor will ever hurt you."

His warmth radiated through my cheek and flowed down the rest of my body, leaving me calm... The way he looked at me, with such concern and protectiveness as he spoke, made me feel like I *could* trust him.

"Okay," I whispered again. "You can't be worse than any other guys I've dated—or I mean, I guess have been on dates with."

"That's my girl." He gave me a small smile. "It's not like you had a choice in the matter either way. That deal you made with the star bound you to me regardless," he said playfully.

I couldn't help but laugh. Great—so apparently *wishing upon a star* had always been code for *making a deal with the devil*. And now? Turns out he has some bizarre, ultra-calming touch. Oh, and he can read my mind. Can't forget that part.

"I can do a lot more than just calm you by touch." He smirked.

I rolled my eyes. This whole alleged mind reading thing was going to get old fast.

So now what? I have a boyfriend from hell?

Chapter 20

Deer

"So, little nightmare—I know that needy little cunt of yours heard my question earlier."

He leaned toward me ever so slightly, placing his hand over mine and guiding it up his thigh slowly.

His filthy words had shocked me before, but hearing them this time stirred something within me. God, this guy could really go from zero to one hundred just like that.

"No God involved here, but you can worship me like one, sweet one." He winked.

I swallowed, feeling the chords of muscle under the thin velvet that covered his thigh. I wasn't sure what to even say. No one has ever talked dirty to me like that, at least not in person. Sure, Felix and I sexted before, very early on in our relationship, but he never said anything even remotely like this face to face.

The corner of his mouth quirked up as he leaned further into me, hand still sliding mine up his thigh.

"Thinking of that feeble man now?" His face was inches from mine, so close I could taste the scent of smoke that seemed to hang around him.

I don't want to fuck him—I don't think? I mean, I think I did just say I'd date him, but fuck him? What are devil dicks even like? Does that even matter in the sense of cock? He's not—not the sexiest man I've ever seen but, I haven't had sex since Felix—and the last time we did that was well over a year ago. Plus, he can't expect me to open my legs up for him just like that! Who does he think I am? I shook the thoughts from my head, suddenly feeling guilty and overwhelmed.

"Calm yourself, little nightmare."

Raios' free hand found my chin and I leaned into the touch, seeking the comfort I knew it could give me. In my movement, I hadn't realized the hand I'd had on his thigh had also moved—and was now resting on the edge of his cock.

I could feel that he was hard—and, from what I could tell, *big*. Instinctively, I slid my hand further up, curious, and gripped him through his pants. A conflicting pulse throbbed between my legs. "Your thoughts are loud, almost insufferably so. So conflicted. —" He brushed his thumb along my bottom lip. "I know that you ache to feel my cock inside you."

Damn him and his mind reading. He pulled my face to his until we were so close our breath intertwined.

"Does it bother you that not only can I speak to your mind, but I can also hear all those pretty little thoughts rolling around in there?" Each word caused his lips to brush against mine.

It didn't bother me so much as it was annoying, knowing every thought I had was on display for the man before me. So much for my previous plan, looks like I was going to have to come to terms with this new reality of mine and just succumb to it. Because I surely wasn't going to give myself up to just being trapped here. Wait, so this meant he *was* able to read my thoughts from the very beginning. That was more embarrassing than anything else!

He moved my hand slowly so that I was now fully stroking him through his pants, a breathy moan escaped his lips. The sound shot a shiver of electricity through me, knowing that such a small guided touch could make someone—something—like him unravel. I rotated my hips forward, pressing my center into the hard wood of the chair. Suddenly desperate for any sort of friction.

"Needy thing you are." He brushed his lips against mine.

Thoughts and worries of Felix faded away, maybe moving on wouldn't be so bad. The gremlin part of my brain piped up—maybe it would make him jealous? But, if I'm stuck down here, would he even know?

Raios growled and pulled away, leaving my mouth cold in his wake.

I stared at him in confusion as he released his hold on me and pushed his chair back leaving me to sit there in sudden embarrassment.

"What is with you and that piss ant of a man?" He growled. "Your thoughts have *perseverated* over that useless waste of breath ever since you moved into that dreadful little apartment building."

I shot him a dirty look and scoffed. His face twisted into a look I was all too familiar with. He couldn't be serious—was he jealous?

"Uh, we dated for years and then he dumped me. I have a right to think about it. It's not my problem that you can read my mind. It's completely reasonable for me to think about him sometimes. Or even wonder and—"

"If you say, miss him..." he warned.

"What does it matter to you if I do or not? It's not like we actually know each other or have *something* between us. We literally just met yesterday!" I raised my voice, gesturing between us as I glared at him.

I folded my arms across my chest.

To think—I actually thought he might be *above* the whole "jealous, unhinged man" thing.

His eyes flared in response.

"Insane? I dragged you to Hell, told you I'm a *devil* and you genuinely thought I was anything but? I'm a literal devil. The first son of the King of Hell, himself. Don't think for one second I am anything *but* insane. And, now that you've agreed to be mine, I will not stand for having my mate think of another man—history or not."

I stared at him, baffled, and barked out a laugh that only seemed to make the flame in his eyes burn hotter.

"*Mate*? I don't even know you! Just because I agreed to go out with you in a moment of—I don't know, *survival*—doesn't mean we're mates, you fucking psycho. I don't care whose son you are—you don't get to tell me who I can or can't think about."

He stormed toward me, but I held my ground, defiant even from my chair. He jabbed a finger into my chest and the spot where he touched me burned.

"We *are* mates. You're mine and I am yours. You made the wish, and I am fulfilling that deal. That mark you now wear on your chest signifies not only the deal, but our bond, don't be such a soft-brained human." He placed his hands on either side of the chair, pushing his weight forward on the arm rests.

"Fuck the mark, fuck your deal, and fuck *you*," I yelled, secretly loving how easy it was to tip him over the edge.

I'd never been one to be confrontational, but something about seeing him so riled up and jealous sparked something in me.

"For as long as your fragile little human heart beats, Deer, you're mine. And the moment that wad of meat stutters and stops in that sultry chest of yours, I'm reclaiming you—remaking you into a demoness to be with me for all eternity."

My head fell back in laughter. Why is it always the hot ones that are insane?

"You crazy son of a bitch."

At least Felix wasn't insane—just an asshole. Raios gripped the arms of the chair so hard the wood splintered between his fingers.

Chapter 21

Deer

"Enough!" he yelled, causing me to jump. "Enough with all the thoughts, and worries for that sorry excuse of a soul." His eyes flared.

I sat, mouth agape, unsure what to do or say. I looked down where the wooden arms of the chair had been—instead, splinters of wood lay in their place. He staggered away from me.

Thinking of Felix really set him off.

"I said, enough!" he roared, kicking the chair he just rose from. "Enough with that man! Camroth, Maldoth!"

Shadows began to pool at his feet as he angrily stalked around the table. I watched as he raised a hand, a small orb of smoke growing from the center of his palm. With a flick of his wrist, he discarded the ball onto the floor. I watched as the smoky orb split into two, growing rapidly in size, reshaping itself, stretching until two oblong shadows the size of men stood before him.

"Mirror!" he yelled at the shadows, as color bled into the darkness.

Cam and Mal emerged from the shifting shadows, both dressed in their sharp crimson suits, carrying a large, circular mirror framed in gleaming gold. Raios didn't turn to look at me as he thrust a finger in my direction. Cam and Mal nodded in silent understanding and began stalking toward me, still carrying the mirror.

"What? Are you going to do some *mirror, mirror on the wall* nonsense now?" I said, watching his shoulder tense at my words. I smirked.

"You torturous little thing. Quiet yourself and watch."

Raios' back was still to me as the twins stood beside me in place of Raios' chair. At first, I thought this was just a sick joke to show me how haggard I looked. My reflection showed my fair, lifeless skin and finger combed red hair. My bloodstained lips looked off-putting in comparison to the pale pallor of my skin—I'd have to confront Raios about that at some point. Hell, it turned out, had terrible lighting.

"Yea, I look like shit. Got it." I quipped.

The mirror began to shimmer, warping my reflection. Images began to form, first as gray undefined shadows until they morphed into... a view of a room?

At first, the image didn't make sense—but then, I caught the familiar half-naked body of Felix stepping from a doorway, rubbing a towel against his hair.

"Felix?" I stared, then looked to Raios, "What is this?"

"Hush up and watch," he commanded, his back still to me.

I shot him a dirty look and sank back into my seat; eyes fixed on the mirror. Felix turned abruptly, as if caught by surprise. But instead of the typical panicked look he wore when something startled him, his face broke out into a wide smile that made my heart ache. I knew that smile—he used to give me that smile every time he saw me, back when we first started seeing each other. Blond hair came into view, and my mouth went dry.

"What...wait." My voice came out breathy and raw.

I wanted to look away, but my eyes wouldn't cooperate, they were pinned to the shit show unfolding before me. I knew that hair. Felix dropped his towel to the floor and opened his arms to the blond.

No. No no no! She slithered into his arms, wrapping hers around his neck to pull him close. My eyes started to burn.

Gracie.

Gracie and Felix?! Is Gracie *sleeping* with Felix?! My insides flipped as my mouth began watering and my stomach threatened to empty its contents onto the floor.

"This—this isn't real," I stammered out. I don't know who I was trying to convince. "This—this you're doing this. That isn't real, *that* isn't real."

My voice shook, well actually, my whole body was vibrating now—he had to be doing this, had to be faking all of it. Regardless, I wouldn't sit and watch this, I *couldn't*.

"No, Deer. I may be able to read your mind and make you wetter than earth's seas, but I can't just conjure shit out of thin air like *that*. That *is* your cohort and your faux-mate defiling your bond. Would you like to see the first time they consummated their deceit and betrayal of you?" Raios asked over his shoulder, still refusing to face me, or even look at me while he spoke. "Or have you had enough?"

From the corner of my eye the images in the mirror began to swirl and shift, disappearing.

"No! No. This is wrong, you're messed up," I yelled at him—at the mirror.

Tears burned my eyes and I gripped my thighs so hard the skin stung. My breathing began to come in short bursts, the wound I had forgotten about for a small while, ripped open.

"Stop muddling your skin with bruises!" Raios was suddenly at my side gripping my wrists. "Enough! You knew deep down—when you made your wish—he was not, *is not,* capable of loving you, let alone ever doing right by your name!"

I fought his grip, tears now pouring from my eyes.

"I've been taking your nightmares for months, all the nightmares of him leaving you. Leaving nothing but the feeling of raw abandonment. *I* took them for you! Do you think that was how I wanted to spend my holiday away from Hell? Falling for some neighboring mortal whose dreams would have sent her into a spiraling depression? No, not really. But I did it anyway. For you."

There was so much anger in his voice—so much that his defense of me started to feel... strange. Disorienting. He fell to his knees beside me, and I realized I was crying. I didn't know when the tears started, but they were like a current of their own.

"Deer," Raios whispered. "I heard you long before that. I listened to you from the deepest pits of Hell—your desperation, sorrow, every shattered birthday wish, every lonely night. I listened for years. Listening to your heartache, it fractured something in me, something I never knew existed."

He pressed his forehead against my shoulder.

"Do you know how long I waited to find the right time to see you? It wasn't just happenstance that I chose Portland, Deer. Years. I spent years watching you decay from neglected love."

I looked at the devil before me and shook my head. The flame in his eyes died down and was replaced by a pain that seemed to match my own. I could hardly process anything he was saying. The only thing I could see, or hear were Gracie and Felix.

His jaw flexed. "Yes, sweet one."

His words were too much—all of this was too much.

I turned my head to stare at the waves of black hair that cascaded over his forehead as his own tears began slipping onto my lap. He turned to look up at me with sorrow-laden eyes.

"I feel what you feel—the anger, fear, sadness, frustrations. All of it, through our bond, through your thoughts," he whispered to me.

I wanted to hate him. I wanted to believe that what I had seen in that mirror was a lie, but part of me knew it was the truth.

Gracie had always gotten everything she wanted with no repercussions—that was crystal clear now. She didn't even seem to care that I had gone missing. She was probably grateful...

"I could kill them," he suggested softly, as he stood and grabbed my arm gingerly. "I could end them, for you."

Well, that's a bit too far. I may hate them right now, Gracie more so than Felix, but I didn't want them *dead*. Karma would eventually catch up with them both.

I stood with him, following his movements mindlessly. He nodded to Cam and Mal who soundlessly began shifting back into shadows, along with the mirror. I didn't care enough to question how that was possible, all I could feel was the sickening pain and betrayal. Nothing else registered. Not that, not Raios' words. Nothing. This break up and birthday surely was one for the books.

Chapter 22
Deer

Raios led me out of the dining hall and down yet another dingy, dark hallway to a slim stairwell that we climbed in silence. His soft grip never relented as we continued, even when we reached the door at the top. He glanced back at me; I didn't need to see him to know his eyes still held the earth's weight in sadness. Why does he even care? Why would anyone like him care about someone like me? I was broken, beat down.

Each step felt like I was climbing a mountain. The last forty-eight hours—the last six months in general, had just utterly drained me. I wanted nothing more than for these feelings to disappear.

The door opened and revealed a low, warmly lit room. A giant four post bed with a black silk canopy sat in its center, surrounded by several fireplaces. A large, darkly themed painting of a broody pond with swans floating on the surface hung above each.

Déjà vu tickled me, but I shoved the feeling away. Who cared?

The room was beyond stuffy and hot, but that didn't matter either. Maybe, if I was lucky enough, the heat would suck the remainder of my life from me. I'd die a heartbroken husk, like a shriveled up human raisin.

Raios quietly guided me through what I assumed to be his room, and sat me on the edge of the bed where he kneeled before me, running his fingers through his hair. I could tell my eyes were beyond swollen from my silent pity fest, the skin around them felt taught and dry.

"Deer, I can be the one for you," he said, almost shyly as he rested his hands on my knees, running his thumbs along the fabric that hung loosely over them. "I *am* the one for you. If you'll allow me to be."

"Yea, because of some twisted deal I didn't know I was making," I murmured, staring down at my feet.

My socks were so beat up and dirty. If I had a shred of dignity left, I'd probably feel self-conscious about them; looking at them now they seemed to reflect what I felt inside.

"No—well, yes, sort of. But no. I could have denied the deal, rejected your sorrowful calls to me. I didn't *have* to go to Portland; I could have chosen anywhere between the three worlds to vacation. I chose you. Without fully knowing you, I chose you."

I heard Raios' words, his confessions, but the meaning didn't really sink in. My mind was a chaotic nest of thoughts—Felix, Gracie, how could they?

"No," Raios said firmly. "Enough of that now."

I wanted to sigh—I knew he was reading my thoughts, sifting through each word that rolled through my head—but I didn't have it in me. I just wanted to let the numbing pain consume me already.

"You mortals are so hardheaded. Stubborn. I can be your happiness, little love. Please allow me to be this for you. You deserve it, no matter what you're feeling right now. You deserve to feel cherished," he proclaimed.

I looked at him again, his eyes were as serious as his tone, and I shrugged.

"Let me be your heaven in these fiery pits, sweet one. Let me take your pain," he coaxed.

The intensity of his gaze nearly stole my breath, for a moment I could feel a flicker of intense affection that didn't seem to come from me, but from what he called our 'bond'.

"Let me take your pain," he offered again. "Give it all to me. Let me hold its weight for you so you never have to bear the burden of heartache, or betrayal ever again."

Take my pain? At this point if he can make these feelings vanish, by all means take it away horn-boy!

He chuckled, clearly the veil of privacy was still thinner than air.

"Why," I croaked, my voice so small and feeble.

There was a pause in his movements as he let out a slow breath.

"Because Deer, I may be a devil but I *am* capable of love," he said carefully, and the word 'love' settled around me like a blanket, the bond between us seemed to vibrate in a way that was impossible for me to understand. "Forfeit your pain, little love. I can handle it. I'll take your pain, and you stay here with me."

I'd forfeit the entirety of my being, if it meant I didn't have to feel this pain anymore.

"Careful with your thoughts right now, sweet one. We're forging a deal that stakes not just your soul, but your entire life as you know it."

Oh. So those weren't just sweet words.

I couldn't help but choke out a hoarse laugh at the seriousness in his tone. It was as if we were *actually* wagering my soul here. I mean, sure let me *'make a deal with the devil'*. Scratch that, let me make *another* deal with the devil. Cue self-loathing eyeroll.

"Whatever you want, I guess. What else do I have to lose? If you can take this feeling away, do it. Hell, if you're that almighty or whatever, take away any trace of Gracie and Felix while you're at it. I can't believe—" he cut me off; his lips pressed softly to mine and my eyes nearly popped out of my head.

Warmth engulfed me, an overwhelming sense of admiration and strength surged through our invisible bond and flowed into me. The tension that had begun cramping my neck eased, and I leaned into the sensation, welcoming the reprieve.

His lips were gentle against mine, each movement of them felt deliberate and downright hypnotizing. The way his tongue slipped along my bottom lip was enough to make me give in.

I leaned into the kiss, the way his mouth tasted like smoke was addicting. His hands slid up my knees to my thighs, gathering my dress in slow, deliberate bunches until they rested firmly on my hips. Through the invisible tether between us, I could feel his yearning, emotions screaming across the bridge that was forming between our hearts. The pain in me dulled, as a reassuring feeling of protection—his protection—took its place. He kissed his way down the side of my cheek and traced my jawline with the tip of his tongue, setting my skin on fire. Each kiss took away more and more of my pain.

His lips found my neck and I couldn't help but moan. It had been so long since someone has kissed me, let alone been intimate with me in any way. His thumbs hooked under the bundled-up hem of my dress and caressed the tops of my thighs. I tensed, anticipation and the need for more building within me.

"You can tell me to stop." The words hung in the air as he placed a delicate kiss on my throat. "At any point, and I will stop."

Not wanting *that* to happen, and feeling the break in woes that I had been longing for, I spread my legs slightly, in the hope that it would be enough reassurance that I wanted this.

He breathed against the column of my throat. "Such a good girl."

I tilted my head back, hoping he would continue those delicious kisses. He took the invitation and swept his tongue up the center of my throat. It was unexpected, and hotter than anything I'd ever experienced. I tilted my hips forward, desperate for friction once more.

"Needy little thing, you are," he purred. "How wet is that cunt of yours?"

It was like flipping a switch with him. One minute he was pissy and yelling, the next he was cooing sweet, filthy nothings at me, and now he's asking about my wet cunt? The word—so vulgar—fell from his lips like poetry. The only thing I could think of was my need to be touched.

"Oh, my sweet nightmare, I'm going to do more than that. I'm going to savor you, every last drop of you. You will scream my name from these infernal pits; all will know you belong to me."

God, I could come from just his words alone at this point. I need him to touch me, but I know I'm not bold enough to make the first move. It's been so long, I feel like I barely know what to do anymore. Felix and I barely ever—the name felt weird in my mind. Almost foreign, my train of thought splintered and suddenly I was left confused about what I'd just been thinking about.

My brows pulled together.

"Stay with me sweet one." Raios slid his thumbs up and brushed along my inner thighs, his mouth working its way deliciously down my chest to the top of my breasts.

"Listen to my voice," he said in my mind, his tone low and sultry—it quickly smothered any fragments of confusion that lingered.

"You're worthy of worship," he muttered against the tops of my breasts, pushing his lips against the low-cut neckline.

I knew I was panting wildly, but I didn't care enough to be self-conscious about my breath. If he didn't touch me, I might lose all sanity. I knew he could hear my thoughts; I could feel his presence in the corner of my mind.

"I need you to say it," he groaned, as he slid his thumb up my thighs, closer and closer to my center.

"I don't know what—" I managed to utter between breaths.

"Say that you are mine." He bit down on the top of my breast so hard it caused me to squeal. His thumb brushed against my throbbing center, causing my breath to hitch.

"I—" I groaned, spreading my legs further for him. "*Please.*" I begged.

"Say it, little nightmare."

He slid his thumb over my clit so lightly it made my head spin. I bucked my hips against the sensation, needing more pressure.

He grinned against my skin before dipping his finger around the edge of my underwear and sliding it softly along my clit.

"I'm yours," I breathed.

The words felt foreign on my tongue, like a betrayal. An image of a man flashed in my mind; his body tangled with a blond. My heart stuttered an aching beat.

"Keep saying it, don't stop."

His thumb slid down to my slit, swiping up and down slowly. I could feel how wet I was for him.

"Sweet one?" he prompted.

"I'm yours," I breathed again and he slipped his thumb inside me.

He pulled away from me slightly, removing his hands from my body, leaving me feeling cold. I looked to him, worried this would be cut short again. I watched as he raised his thumb to his lips, the skin shined with my arousal as he ran his tongue over it.

Heat flushed my cheeks as his eyes locked with mine, darkening with a need that mirrored my own. "Again," he commanded.

"I'm yours," I repeated, the verse felt more natural in my mouth this time.

Raios wasted no time pushing his hand back to the spot between my thighs. With his thumb, he pushed my underwear to the side, then pressed a finger inside me, immediately working my pussy with slow, deliberate strokes.

Chapter 23

Raios

I could feel her pain ebb away with each pump of my finger. The way her pussy pulsed around me made my mouth water. The taste of her wetness lingered on my tongue, and it took everything in me not to shove her back and suck her soul through that wet, beautiful cunt of hers.

I curled my finger inside her, pressing on that specific spot that made human women go berserk. Maybe I could just have one lick. I wanted to feel her soft clit on my tongue—just for a second.

I dipped my head between her thighs, using my free hand to pull the fabric that covered her center to the side, pinning it against her thigh.

The moan that left my little nightmare's mouth after the first swipe of my tongue was nearly enough to make me cum then and there. Hell, she was divine. And that fucker neglected her? Maybe I'll kill him. It had been a while since I tortured someone for leisure—the sound of my name leaving her lips snapped me out of the thought.

I jerked my head up, nearly startled to hear such ravenous, sultry beauty wrapped around my name. Her head was tilted back, and I could feel her pussy throbbing around my finger.

My nightmare is close.

"Do you want me to make you come, sweet one?" I purred to the mortal little hellhound grinding against my touch.

"Yes," she moaned. "Please."

"Who do you belong to?" I coaxed.

"You. I'm yours Raios—"

I dipped my head back between her thighs, lapping at her clit—slow, deliberate strokes of my tongue, sucking and twirling around that sensitive little spot.

It was easy for me to know how to please her, all it took was a small peek into her mind to know where she needed to be touched.

"I'm yours, I'm yours, *I'm yours—*"

The words tore from her lips like a forbidden hymn as her orgasm ripped through her, raw and divine. I felt her soul seep into mine, our deal locking into place—sealed in pleasure and power. I smirked against her cunt.

Chapter 24

Raios

Deer collapsed onto my bed, her chest rising and falling in deep, measured breaths. *Good.* I let my shadows explore every corner of her mind. No memories of that bastard and bitch remained, just the essence of a forgotten memory. I knew her memories of them would resurface again, at some point, but I couldn't tell her that. She needed this, and I needed to show her that even when those memories came back, she no longer needed anything like that, or them, in her life.

I shrugged my approval, *that should be fine enough.* I needed her to be mine. Fully.

I couldn't rule Hell without a mate. But what compelled me to choose a mortal? I had no idea. I didn't even know what they required in their fragile bonds. Maybe it was her fractured heart—ripe for the taking, making her an easy target. The broken ones were always the easiest for making deals, desperation typically greased that wheel.

What I hadn't anticipated, was feeling anything real for her. That part came as a complete surprise.

It was about three years ago when I had first heard her heartbroken wail in my mind. It was the first time that pig of an ex-boyfriend and her had fought. The names he called her, the way he dismissed her, it left me wanting to send a demon up there to ruin him wholly.

She'd pleaded with God that night—bargaining with him, offering to become a better person, in return for Him fixing her slowly deteriorating relationship with that failure of a man.

I listened to her thoughts nightly after that—almost as if it were an addiction. Soon after, I began to take her nightmares from her. Her waking life was filled with enough pain. I couldn't bear the thought of allowing her sleeping life to be equally so. It became my own selfish mission, from then on, to make her mine—to show her what love *could* be like.

Human love was so fickle, but love from an Underworlder? *That* was damn near an entity of its own.

Having not known that they didn't have bonds, but instead bizarre relationship habits that were more or less just drawn-out courting rituals ending in marriage, this was likely going to be a long game. It seemed like a waste of time to me, and despite how much I hoped that when she woke up, she'd be ready to take on her role of Queen so we could get straight to ruling, I knew it could be a slower build to win her love—deal or not—but I needed to expedite that process.

Changes needed to be made in Hell. Father's reign has been sloppy—demons left and right were slipping through the cracks and fucking shit up, up north.

I had no idea how long I watched her sleep. Not knowing how much sleep mortals required, I was unsure if this amount was excessive or not. I watched as her breasts rose and fell, taunting me with each shallow breath. Part of me wondered how she'd react if I woke her up with my face between those perfect thighs. My cock throbbed at the thought.

Next thing I knew my cock was in my hand as I stroked myself, thinking of the woman who had haunted my nightmares.

Chapter 25
Deer

The bed rocked gently as I woke—a raspy moan made its way to my ears. My tired brain fought to clear the confusion that had taken residence there. I felt hollow inside—as if some part of me was missing, or I had forgotten something important. It felt like when you leave the house in a rush and can't remember if you unplugged your hair straightener, or shut off the oven.

A grunt beside me followed by heavy panting convinced me to lift my head from the bundle of covers I had burrowed beneath.

Raios sat beside me, sweat kissing his skin. He appeared almost pearlescent now, his skin a soft shade of gray I hadn't noticed before. Maybe it was the lighting from the fireplaces. I watched as his arm began moving erratically by his side, almost as if he was—

"Are you seriously jacking off next to me while I sleep?"

I all but screamed at him, slamming my hand down on the puff of blanket blocking my view. As angry as I pretended to be, my curiosity still got the best of me. Fuck it—if he was bold enough to stroke himself next to me, then of course I was going to take a peek.

Can't say I minded that I did.

My eyes locked on his cock as his fist pumped hard around it. I could confidently say I'd never seen a gray cock before—darker than his skin, slick and smooth, like it would feel like silk against my tongue.

"Deer," he moaned as he slowed his strokes.

Something about the way he said my name made my pussy throb—I suddenly craved to hear my name fall from those hellish lips as I rode him.

"Do you want me to stop?" he asked.

I shook my head, unable to peel my eyes away.

"Come here," he whispered, as he switched hands—opening his side to me.

Something about this felt strange, not quite wrong—but also not quite right.

Less than twenty-four hours ago, he showed up knocking on my door, locked out of his house. Then, he stole me away, and now...well, now I was laying in his bed, watching him touch himself.

I crawled up to his side, my dress beyond disheveled and wrinkled from the night. He turned his head toward me and kissed my cheek, his lips lingering as he spoke huskily, "You're devastating."

"So you've said." I rolled my eyes, and he chuckled against my skin.

"Do you like watching me touch myself to you?" His lips brushed my skin, and I nodded wordlessly.

"Say it, sweet one."

"I like it," my voice felt small, and he chuckled again.

"Would you like to feel how my cock feels inside of you?" He smiled against my neck, and I gulped, nodding again.

"So shy, little love. No need for that." He let go of his cock, and it bounced in the air, throbbing.

He gently pushed my side, inviting me to crawl on top of him. Slowly, I climbed onto him, bundling my dress at my hips as I hovered above him. The heat radiating from his center sent a shiver through my body.

Raios' hands slipped under the cut of my dress and found the sides of my underwear. With a quick tug, they tore from my body. I stared at him baffled.

"Hey!"

"Don't worry, we'll get you stocked up on clothing later today, sweet one."

His lower lip pulled between his teeth, his lust-laden eyes hypnotizing. I could hardly make sense of anything he was saying, the only thing on my mind was what that heat would feel like inside me.

"You don't have to do this, if you don't want to," he said, squeezing my hips reassuringly. "You will not offend me if you crawl off of me."

No.

I lowered myself on him, my pussy gently brushing the heat of his cock. I half expected it to sizzle. The feeling was divine; unlike anything I'd ever felt. He growled, and the sound vibrated through my core. I needed more of that delicious sound.

I placed my hands on his shoulders as I slid my wetness along the length of his shaft—all the way to the tip and back. I continued to do so until the sound of his growls filled the room.

"Little nightmare," he ground out, as his head fell back from pleasure. "I have to tell you—"

I reached between our bodies and fisted his cock before sliding the tip of it along my slit. His hips bucked in response.

"*Deer*," he moaned—that sound was enough to shatter my resolve, making me lower myself fully onto him. I sent up a silent prayer that he wouldn't rip me open.

"Yes, Raios, what did you need to tell me?" I purred sweetly.

His grip tightened on my waist as he went completely still. Oh, maybe he wasn't as into this, or me, as I thought.

"*No!* Don't think that," he managed to pant out. "Don't think that, even for one second." His eyes met mine, worry lacing his crimson irises.

"It's just...I have never, you know..." he trailed off as he glanced down to where our bodies connected.

Confusion knitted my brows as I struggled to fill in the blanks. He sighed, forcing his eyes closed and tilting his head back.

"Deer, I haven't ever been with anyone. Not like this, at least." The words rushed out of him and I couldn't hide my surprise.

"Seriously?"

The moment the question left my mouth; regret slammed into me. *That* is not something you ask when someone tells you they are a virgin.

"Yes," he admitted, eyes glued to a mystery spot on the ceiling. "I understand if that makes you not want to uh—not want to continue. I get it and I will not be offended."

My guilt worsened.

"No," I grabbed his face between my hands and pulled gently so that he had to look at me. "I'm sorry, I was just surprised, is all. I figured, with you know, how you look and how good you are at everything, how much you asked for my consent—" I shrugged.

I began to pull away from him, the feeling that I'd completely spoiled the mood settling in.

"You did no such thing. I want this, if you want this. I want you, all of you, in every sense of the words."

"Are you sure you want to lose your virginity, to *me*? I'm just a human, not even the hottest human." I laughed, trying to make light of the awkward situation.

"You are not *just* a human. You are my mate. I chose *you*, and I will forever choose you. I hope someday you'll feel the same for me."

The intense look in his eyes was so genuine and so serious it made me want to look away, but I didn't.

I'd been love bombed before. This sort of felt like that but also felt very different. Granted everything about this felt very different.

"I only want to do this if you do, sweet one," he whispered.

I nodded and did the only thing that felt right in the moment—I leaned forward and kissed him. His lips were gentle against mine, as he kissed me softly and slowly. His hands pressed gently on my hips and I reached between our bodies to grab his cock again. This time as I rubbed his tip along my slit, I lowered myself ever so slightly, so that he entered me further with each pass.

"Deer," he moaned into my mouth.

The sultry sound of my name slipping from his mouth made me shiver, and I lowered myself until he filled me completely. My body took a moment to adjust to his size, as the ungodly heat from his cock radiated through me. I began rocking my hips slowly, wanting to savor every second of this feeling, I couldn't help but moan at the movement. His cock felt too good. I gripped his shoulders as his grip on my hips grew tighter while he guided me to a pace that suited his needs.

"Little nightmare," he growled, biting down on his lower lip.

"Is this okay?" I panted.

I lowered my head beside his and his breath filled my ear.

"Perfect, you're such a good girl," he breathed, pulling me along him faster as my breath hitched. "You are perfect for me. Do you feel how hard I am? That's all because of you, every inch of me is yours."

I moaned and dug my fingers into his shoulders.

"That's it little love, ride your mates' cock. I want to feel that cunt of yours tighten around my cock as you cum. I want to hear you cry out my name. Look at me, love."

His hand left my hip and pulled my face gently in front of his. I tried to avert my gaze but his growl told me I should do otherwise. His eyes were rimmed with emotion and lust, and so red it was like looking into the heart of a flame.

"I want you to look at me while you cum."

His pace quickened as he pulled me down onto him by my hips. He felt so good—almost too good. This was the kind of sex I had always craved. Intimate and hot.

Pressure began to build in the pit of my stomach and my skin began to tingle as I could feel my climax building.

"Please, cum for me, Deer."

He pressed our foreheads together, eyes never leaving mine. It felt strange being eye to eye with someone like this, but it was also the hottest thing I had ever experienced.

"That's it love, don't stop."

My movements became erratic as I ground my pussy against his body, his cock filling me with the most delicious friction and pressure imaginable. I moaned and closed my eyes as another growl escaped him, causing me to snap them back open.

"Eyes on me," he commanded. "Cum for me, like you love me."

Before his command registered, the world around me shattered. The strongest orgasm of my life rocked through me. My legs quivered as I bucked against him, my pussy begged for a break, but Raios would not allow me that.

He moaned so softly that it rekindled the fire within me as I watched the devil beneath me melt and groan.

"*Deer*," he moaned my name—the sound sweeter than the darkest honey.

He removed his hand from my face and placed it directly onto my chest between my breasts, right above my heart as his eyes found mine.

I mustered up the last few ounces of energy, trying to ignore how sensitive I was, and rode him hard. Each thrust caused the wooden posts of his bed to grate against the stone floor. He freed my hip to grab my hand off his shoulder and press my palm to his chest, mimicking his—my hand sat directly over the devil's heart and I could feel the thunderous beat it produced.

I watched him and felt his heartbeat as he came undone. His eyes never left mine even as they softened and squinted while he came deep inside of me. His cum felt like fire swirling inside me—it was alarming for a moment, but was also strangely sexy and pleasant.

"I will never discard you, Deer. I will never turn my back on you and make you wonder why you were not enough. I will fulfill every wish you have and rebuild your heart piece by piece if I have to. I will show you what love truly is like. And, if the day ever came when you were somehow no longer in my grasp, I would tear through the fabric of time and reality to find you. You are mine, and I am yours."

I blinked at his words, speechless from the proclamation, and it was as though I could feel a piece of my broken heart snapping back into place.

He may have been a devil, but he fucked like a god.

Chapter 26

Deer

My head was on the devil's chest, I had no idea how long we had been like that, but somehow it felt like home. Nothing made sense—yet, lying here with him felt *right*. I couldn't discern my exact feelings for him, but I no longer felt the urge to flee.

"How are you feeling?" he asked.

"I feel...good. Nice," I said, and shrugged.

I honestly didn't know how I was feeling, all I knew was that I didn't feel bad. I couldn't share that I felt like a part of me was missing, that seemed to me like it would be a mood killer. Besides, I knew he already knew exactly how I felt, on account of the mind reading.

"You feel nice?" He laughed.

"Yes, I feel *nice*." I chuckled along with him.

"So, are you...really?" I wasn't exactly sure how to ask the question.

"Is it not obvious by the horns? Yes, sweet one. I'm a devil."

Looks like I didn't have to know how to ask it after all. He laughed, probably at the randomness of my question.

I shrugged. "Hey man, I don't know. We were in Portland after all. So like, it's a valid question."

"Does that not freak you out?"

"What? That you're a devil? Well, yeah. It does—it did, I guess. But now, not so much. I don't know what changed my mind, but it's kind of hot. The whole devil thing. Besides, you're pretty decent for a devil." I glanced up at him and winked.

"Well, so long as you think I'm *decent* then." He laughed and kissed the top of my head before gesturing to the room we were in. Surrounded by several fireplaces and rough stone walls. "And this?"

"And this what? Your room?"

He shrugged. "Yeah."

Talk about awkward pillow talk.

I shrugged again. "I don't know. It's your room, so I don't feel my opinion of it matters?"

"True, but this is also to be your room. We are in Hell. We're *in* Hell. *This* is Hell," he said with a tone so serious; I couldn't help but laugh. "And granted, to me, this is comfortable. I want *you* to be comfortable as well and I want you to enjoy the spaces we will share."

When I didn't stop laughing, he said, "I'm serious."

This all should have sent me on a downward spiral, but I couldn't stop laughing. Tears began pooling in the corners of my eyes, and apparently, my fit of giggles was contagious, because Raios began to laugh too.

And, *that* sound? Worlds better than his moan.

"You're so weird," I wheezed between laughs.

I looked up at him and watched as the corners of his eyes crinkled and his laughter vibrated off the stone walls.

"What?" he asked, wiping the corner of his eye. "What is so *weird* about wanting my mate to be comfortable in her space?"

I rolled my eyes at his words.

"Who said I'd stay here?"

"First off, you did, when you came for me. Second, you don't have a choice, considering our deal now, little love." He chuckled again.

Oh, right. That. Would I really be okay with staying here in Hell? What would I even do here?

"You're staring," he cooed, and brushed his thumb along my cheek.

I shrugged, "you're insane but beautiful—I mean, your laugh is beautiful."

He rolled his eyes. "Well sweet one, you're insane for suddenly being fine with the whole *abduction to hell, fucking a devil* thing."

Was I fine with this whole situation? I wasn't *not* fine about it, I felt finer about this than anything else recently.

I shrugged and smiled. "Yeah, bat-shit insane I guess."

Truth is, if I really sat with these emotions, the reality was I hadn't felt this happy in a long time. Sure, this happiness was given to me by a legitimate devil from Hell, but it was happiness nonetheless. That, and I actually felt sexy and worthy of someone's time, for once.

His smile faltered. "You will always be worthy of me. I will worship you until the stars fall from the sky and consume all the worlds, little love."

I groaned. "Will there ever be a day where you're not eavesdropping on my thoughts?"

"Oh, I'm always listening, little love," he winked, "and I always will be."

"And what's with all the pet names?"

"Pet names—for my pet," he said with a mock frown. "You don't like them?"

I elbowed him in his side playfully, and he clutched it with a fake yelp.

"Such brutal strength for such a small mortal," he groaned, pretending to double over in pain. "The agony! I think you've broken a rib!"

"Oh, shut up!" I giggled.

Mortal. The word stuck out to me. *If he's calling me a mortal, does that mean he's not?* Something about that made my heart ache.

"Enough of that, Deer. I will outlive you technically, yes—but I will not allow you to die without me. We are in this for eternity; besides, Death is a close friend of mine." He winked. "Once bound, always bound."

I chewed the inside of my lip. It wasn't like I was going to die soon; I was only twenty-five. But the thought was a buzzkill nonetheless.

"Come on, you, we need to get up and get you something." He moved to slide off the bed and part of me wanted to yank him back. "We should get you some clothes and whatever else you may need. Some food, perhaps?" He stretched.

"I only really need another pair of underwear—and something other than a dress would be nice. It's not like I need *clothes* clothes." I looked up at him. "There's food in Hell?"

He looked surprised by my question. "Gluttony is a sin, baby. We got it all here." He winked again.

"Come, I'll show you. You're in for a treat, if there's one thing I know about humans, it's that your idea of Hell is outlandishly far from the reality." He raised an eyebrow playfully. "You're here to stay, sweet one. That was the deal you made, you're mine, love. You will get all the same perks I do, my future Queen."

Something twisted in my stomach at those words—*Queen.* Maybe living in Hell wouldn't be so bad.

Wait. "Work—" I blurted out.

"Work?"

"Yeah, work. It's a thing us *humans* do to survive. I can't just leave my career..." I waved my hand above my head, causing Raios to sneer.

He knelt on the side of the bed and ran a finger over my chest.

"The mark on your skin is a symbol of our bond. It's our symbol that we own each other, you own all that I own. You will never have to *work* to survive, love," he said, caressing the raised skin I had forgotten about.

That's right. Something burned my chest before, but I was too distracted to consider what it had been, let alone inspect it.

"But still, I—I'm a writer. I can't just give up on my work. I've spent my whole life writing and building my reader community—"

He tilted his head to the side.

"Ah, your *passion.* Well, just tell me what you need and I'll make it happen." He nodded.

"Also, what do you mean we own each other?" I was beginning to panic. "I don't really remember our deal—"

"It's a bond...we mate for life down here. You can think of it as me being your boyfriend, if that's easier." He leaned down and kissed my forehead.

"It's not as scary as it sounds, and the scar of the bond is hardly visible to the naked eye. It feels more raised than it is—it's fresh. After a few days, you'll barely be able to notice it at all."

The word *boyfriend* struck a chord in my brain, and suddenly fragments of what initiated the deal flashed through my mind. I couldn't quite pinpoint the cause, but I could recall the raw feeling of desperation and heartbreak.

"Come on, I'll explain while we're at the market. We really *do* need to get you some new clothes."

Chapter 27

Raios

How could I be so daft?

Of course, she would want to carry on with her mundane tasks here. If she wanted to continue to write, I guess that wasn't so bad. She could easily do that while ruling beside me—granted, her role was more so just her being there for me.

I pondered what roles would be best suited for her—perhaps she could look after a few of the districts? It was hard to say what she'd enjoy doing down here. I supposed this would be a better conversation to have with her, rather than me making meek assumptions. I wanted her to be my equal. I wanted her to *feel* like my equal.

She gasped, pulling me out of my stream of thoughts. When I looked down at her, her jaw was nearly on the ground. I followed her surprised stare and spotted a demon just a few paces in front of us and chuckled.

"Don't worry," I whispered down to her as I pulled her under my arm. "Nothing and no one will ever hurt you down here."

She looked up at me with eyes as wide as saucers, the expression in her eyes begged me to sift through her thoughts—but I'd been trying to refrain. She didn't outwardly seem bothered by me reading her thoughts so openly, but there was a part of her that found it annoying.

Annoying her was the last thing I wanted to do; I didn't want to push her away. If anything, I wanted to pull her in as close as she'd allow—which, based on the tidbits I *did* have the pleasure of sneaking out of her mind, she wanted the same.

I couldn't help but grin at the realization that she actually did like me—which earned me a confused look from her.

"What?" she mused, squinting her eyes at me.

"Nothing!" I grinned wider and laughed.

"No, it's something. What is it?"

She narrowed her glare, a clear attempt at being intimidating, but I could see the light in her eyes dancing.

"Nothing, I like you. I like having you here, at my side."

I shrugged, feeling the heat rising to my cheeks. I cringed internally, did I just say that? What a damned cheese ball.

She laughed and leaned into me, her smile was warm and nothing short of lovely.

"Who knew devils could be so sweet," she teased, as she squeezed my arm. "I *might* like you too."

She rolled her eyes and I breathed a sigh of relief; I didn't need to check her mind to know she meant what she said. I could feel her warmth and affection sing through the bond. It made my heart happy, knowing I could bring her even a morsel of joy, this is all I had wanted for us—for her.

"Hmm, enough to dwell in the fiery pits of Hell with me for all of eternity?" I asked theatrically, as we passed a group of Underworlders who gave me an odd look—quickly snuffing it out as my eyes met theirs.

They knew better than to judge me, or anything I was doing. I could make their lives quite literal Hell, if I so pleased. Though, I did like Hell being more of a place of comfort for my people.

In all fairness, I hardly ever went out in public like this. I had always spent my time in my home. On rare occasions, I'd surfaced up top when I needed a break from here—the gaping stares were warranted, I'd be the same way if I saw my ruler casually walking about, I'm sure—but it all made me self-conscious, like a spectacle.

Chapter 28

Deer

Boutiques lined the center of the market square, no different from a typical outdoor mall. I was stunned. I hadn't known what to expect when he said we'd go shopping—call me whatever you'd like, but I fully expected something out of a horror movie. Yet everything here, so far, had been almost normal. It all resembled home, with the exception of the occasional demon strolling past us and giving a nod to Raios.

The demons here looked like regular people, save for the occasional tail or tattered wing, and unexpectedly seemed fairly kind.

From what I gathered, Hell seemed to be split into seven sectors—following the seven deadly sins or something like that, I wasn't sure. I never paid much mind to anything in the realm of religion before, so I had taken to absorbing each bit of information, one morsel at a time.

All of the sectors seemed to surround a single hub, which also coincidentally was where Raios' home was. I had expected, upon exiting his place, I'd discover we'd been in a castle of sorts—or a really nice cave. I definitely didn't expect to find that it was a really nice, well-kept estate. Pride was his family's sector, yet we were currently in the Greed district.

My mind kept slipping back to the things he had said before in his room about the deal and the bond—owning each other—as we strolled down the peculiar commercial strip of shops. I didn't dislike the thought at all, not when I really sat with my emotions. Even back at my apartment, something about him just felt right. I liked the way he talked to me and how, when he looked at me, he did so as if I were the most prized possession in his life. Sure, I still felt like something was missing inside me—maybe it was the bond burned into my chest talking—but I felt more myself here than I think that I ever had back home.

"Don't worry about paying for anything, everyone knows we're together." Raios slung his arm across my shoulder as we walked into one of the shops. "Being the Prince of Hell has its perks."

"Ah, Prince! Excellent to see you," an elderly man with weathered gray skin said, smiling warmly at Raios. "What can I do for you today?"

Raios gestured to me. "Whatever she wants, put it under my name."

I glanced at the man and gave him an awkward smile and he smiled warmly in return.

"Of course, Prince. Whatever you wish."

Raios turned to me. "So, what would you like to look for first? Lingerie perhaps?" His smile was so captivating it made my breath stutter.

I rolled my eyes. "Sure, *Prince*. Maybe the old man can help me dress and all."

He huffed a laugh and pulled me in close to his side. It felt intimate and roused the lazy butterflies that had barely gone dormant in my stomach.

"Over my dead body," he chuckled, kissing the top of my head.

With Raios' arms stacked high with various items, I felt satisfied with my haul. I couldn't believe I was really here to stay. Deal or not, I mean, Hell sounded awful and the thought of *choosing* to live in Hell sounded insane. But all things considered it really, wasn't bad at all—nothing like I had always imagined. Things could only go up from here (literally).

We ended our adventure in the Gluttony seated on the rooftop of some lavish restaurant where, to no one's surprise, Raios had his own table with the best view.

The server placed our food in front of us, two normal—not Hell-ish looking—burgers. Mine, without ketchup, of course, and Raios' surprisingly with no condiments at all. Who would have thought the next ruler of Hell hated pickles?

I grinned at him over my burger.

"What?" He eyed me suspiciously.

"Nothing," I smiled and bit into my food, which just so happened to be the best thing I had ever eaten.

Raios picked off a corner of his bun and popped it into his mouth.

"You know I can just read your mind to find the answer—"

I rolled my eyes. "Lest I forget the all-powerful spawn of the big Underworlder himself can read minds."

He bit into his burger, eyes still sizing me up.

"This is our first date," I said, as I wiped the corner of my mouth.

His eyes glittered. "Oh, so you didn't count me abducting you and dragging you to Hell as our first date? Not even the nightmare of a dinner with my parents? Shocking."

I kicked him lightly under the table, grateful the new shoes I'd gotten were extremely comfortable. I glanced down, making sure I hadn't scuffed them from the kick. "No, Raios. Taking me from my home and *licking* my tears did not count as a first date, nor did your mother verbally attacking me."

"What was I supposed to do? Invite you to Hell? Much more memorable to be dragged here instead."

"Yea, much more *dramatic.*"

"Are you implying you would have come with me freely if I had just invited you?"

"No," I barked out. "I would have called you crazy and told you to fuck off."

"Exactly, so—" He grabbed the ornate glass of water in front of him and raised it for a toast. "To first dates—sans abduction—and shitty mothers!"

I grinned and huffed a laugh, raising my burger in the air. "To first dates, sans licking each other's tears!"

With a stomach full of the best burger I'd ever eaten and a new wardrobe, it was safe to say that this had been the best date of my life—which, come to think of it, was kind of pitiful.

We entered the Pride district and the lack of Underworlders was peculiar, but to be expected. Raios explained to me that his family and him were essentially royalty, hence why Cam and Mal and so many others referred to him as *Prince*. Come to think of it, I hadn't seen them since I'd arrived.

"Cam and Mal don't live here with you?" I asked, as he linked his arm with mine while we walked to his estate. "Do they live nearby?"

He tilted his head at me, scanning my face.

"Cam and Mal? Why are you curious about them? They're essentially, nothing."

Well, that was rude. He grinned and shook his head, raising his free hand.

I watched as smoke formed in the center of his palm.

"I can control shadow, it's weaker right now, believe it or not. It will be stronger when I take over as leader—*King*." He winked at the word. "Look."

I eyed his palm skeptically as the ball of shadow writhed against his hand and split, reshaping into two small figures that materialized as miniature versions of Cam and Mal, and gasped.

Ah, I'd seen him do this before. I felt a flush of embarrassment for asking—if I'd just given the thought an ounce of effort, I would have remembered that he'd made them appear out of thin air before. Raios abruptly stopped walking, causing me to stumble over my own feet.

"Don't think like that. Your curiosity is valid. You'll have many questions about things here as our time together continues. Do not ever feel like you can't or shouldn't ask me things."

He brought his hand down to my eye level. "I created them when I was a kid—I was lonely. Not many demons or others here want to be friends with the son of...well," he gestured around us. "It has a certain stigma to it."

"But everyone we saw today was so friendly toward you, I can't imagine they would have treated you any differently as a kid?"

"Deer, they're *respectful* toward me. They fear me."

I was quiet for a moment, watching Cam and Mal walk along their creator's palm. My mind spun with hundreds of questions about the tiny figures.

"They're sentient in the sense that they're tiny pieces of me, but don't worry. They feel no pain unless I feel it, so there's no way to harm them. They've kept me company for years, I honestly don't know how I would have survived by myself if I hadn't created them."

I looked up at the devil who was wrapped around my arm, spilling bits of his insecurities to me. Pain colored his eyes as he stared down at his not so imaginary-imaginary friends.

"Honestly, they were the *only* thing I had until now."
Then it struck me, he had been inconceivably lonely.

Chapter 29

Deer

We spent hours walking his grounds, the air was filled with stories of his childhood. How isolated he had been, and how woefully lonely it all had been. His father was never around—always too busy with meetings, reigning in his demons, and organizing newcomers. His mother sounded like she had always been a bitch and he always hated her role here, so it was no surprise to hear she was hardly a mother to him at all.

It hurt my heart to hear all of it, and it made me look at him in a different light. No one's childhood was sunshine and rainbows; we all had our own baggage of sorts. I felt for him. Granted, my childhood wasn't necessarily like his, but I had always been in the shadow of others. Only ever having one friend, who for one reason or another no longer seemed to matter to me—no seriously, it was like all emotions towards her were removed from me. When I thought about us growing up together, I knew I had loved her—knew she was my best friend. But now, when I thought about her, it was like a hollow spot in my heart had been carved out where she used to be, and it didn't even bother me.

Raios tugged on my arm, pulling me from my thoughts.

"Come on sweet one, it's getting late and you need proper sleep. Tomorrow we will make the room more to your liking."

Chapter 30

Raios

I lowered my lips to her forehead and pulled the blankets up around her; she had fallen asleep so fast. The first day here had really taken a lot out of her, but I was pleasantly surprised to find she was adjusting well. At first, I thought it was going to be impossible to get her to like it here—let alone to like me. But every corner of her mind held my name and I wouldn't want it any other way.

Exiting my room, I conjured Cam and Mal, dumping them from my palm onto the floor.

The shadow twins stood before me and Mal nodded his head to me.

"Alright boys." I walked between them and wrapped my arms around their shoulders, "Listen close."

I sent the twins to the Rivers Styx; I needed them to go up top for a few necessities. This had to be perfect. I spent the last two hours clearing out a spare room in the estate, and scouring Deer's brain as she slept—making sure no nightmares crept through the cracks.

The room was a hair larger than mine; the walls lined with empty shelves that previously held my father's tomes. By previously, I mean I carried every single one out and piled them into my mother's wardrobe room. Those dusty, unread things could be her problem—it's not like father ever read them to begin with.

I took special care to make sure every speck of dust, every cobweb, and every hell spider was eradicated from the space—before I lit all five of the fireplaces to warm the room. I had about six more hours until Deer would likely wake up, and this needed to be perfect for her.

Mal appeared beside me, causing me to jump and I shot him a glare.

He sneered, as he adjusted the large cardboard box in his arms.

"Where's—"

Cal appeared beside him and I rolled my eyes. He dropped the box at my feet, such an ornery bastard, he could be.

"Would it kill you to be careful," I scoffed and he rolled his eyes.

"I wish," he quipped in reply.

I should have done better when I created him. When I was a kid, I didn't know creating minions such as them would spawn from parts of my emotions.

Mal placed his box beside Cams, and we began sifting through the contents.

Chapter 31
Deer

"Little love," Raios whispered sweetly in my ear and I burrowed deeper into the soft, warm bed.

He reached under the covers, grabbed me by the waist and squeezed. The pajamas he bought for me yesterday were so soft combined with how plush his bed was, it felt like I was in heaven.

"Oh, is that so?" He purred; his warm hands sliding beneath the edge of my shirt and trailing up my ribs.

"Do I need to drag you out of bed, little love?" he mused, as he trailed a finger along the bottom of my breast, my skin tightening under his touch.

"What's the rush?" I groaned, ignoring the heat building between my thighs, and peeked out from beneath the blankets at Raios.

My eyes skimmed over him, his hair was slicked back, taut against his head and he wore a loose, black canvas jacket—strangely casual and dare I say, human?

The corner of his mouth curved into a smirk as my eyes trailed down his charcoal gray covered chest and he tilted his head, a rogue piece of hair slipped out and fell across his forehead.

"I have a gift for you," he said, as he continued trailing his finger along my skin. "But if you'd rather skip the present and do something a little more—" he paused and leaned close to brush his lips lightly against mine.

"Then I suppose it could wait." He pulled back and sighed dramatically.

The man was driving a hard bargain. I was craving the feeling of his cock in me again, and direly wanted to know what he would feel like slamming into me from behind. However, he had a surprise for me and that had me curious.

I narrowed my eyes at him, curiosity overriding my need for cock and sighed.

"Alright, alright. Fine."

I scooted out from under his touch and the covers to stand beside him. He was watching me expectantly.

"What?" I asked.

"Well, now I'm nervous," he said shyly and ran his fingers through his hair, disheveling the orderly strands.

"You? A wicked, nefarious devil, nervous?" I balked. "Now, that's a first." I playfully batted his arm.

He really was a timid, shy thing—for the most part. Mainly when it came to things he felt were sentimental, it seemed. I had only been here for maybe a hair over twenty-four hours (who knows, there were no clocks in Hell, go figure), but from what I'd gathered so far it didn't really seem like he had any experience in the dating world.

A twinge of jealousy hit me, as I realized that he may not have had dating experience but he for sure had experience in *other* things—that much was evident, right? He had to have at the very least fooled around with others before me.

I waited for him to tell me to 'stop thinking about such things' but he said nothing.

My sudden excitement and arousal were almost immediately soured after that fun little thought. How many people had he messed around with before me? (Women, demons, a secret third option I don't know of?) He was pretty damn skilled with those fingers and tongue, so I had to assume it was quite a few. Plus, with how hot he was, there's no way that number would be small. He had mentioned that he was spending his holiday from Hell in Portland—and believe me when I say, that city wasn't having a shortage on attractive women.

"Deer?" He chirped, I hadn't realized he was standing with his hand outstretched to me.

Reluctantly I slid my hand into his, unable to stop the slew of shitty thoughts. He led us to the door. I didn't care much for the stairs that led up to his room, let alone the hallways in general—or really much else in the estate, honestly. The hallways were creepy, and I didn't like the fact that if I wanted to walk around by myself, the odds of them doing whatever fuckery they did before, when one of the twins pushed me out the door, were high. I'd have to make a point to ask Raios about that, because if I was really going to stay here, I didn't want to play whatever game this weird-ass, suspiciously sentient house was playing.

My thoughts from before—Raios' extracurricular activities that had clearly helped him hone his maddeningly good fingerbanging skills—resurfaced. The jealousy it stirred in me had me second-guessing if I could actually stay here. Not that I ultimately had a choice, considering I'd forfeited whatever fraction of my soul to him when we were bound, blah-blah-blah. But maybe I could at least see if I could get my own space somewhere else in the Pride district. I hated this all-too-familiar sense of feeling less-than. The looming feeling that he's potentially—likely—been with someone much more attractive than me, was such a familiar pain, one would think I'd have been numb to it by now.

Raios sighed beside me. "Listen, I'm trying to be respectful of your mind and not listen in on your thoughts but I picked up on the fact that that bothers you, but Deer—" He paused on a step, tugging me gently to a stop with him.

He regarded me, his stare intense. "No one that I've been with before you matters—not in the slightest. I will reassure you with every breath if need be if that is what it takes to make sure that you know where you stand with me, and in my life now. I understand this situation is fast, atypical, and a multitude of other things, but you are mine and I am yours." He grinned slyly.

"Besides, no one that has ever mattered in my life has met my parents." He winked.

I had forced that whole interaction from my mind, it was unpleasant to say the least. But his words stitched together a few more pieces of my poor, broken heart. It was reassuring to know where I stood with him, circumstances aside—it meant a lot hearing him say that.

"Oh, and I will see to it that you are able to roam freely without the house doing...what it does. We will also make the place more to your liking. This is your home too."

We continued on in comfortable silence. I swore that if it wasn't for the fact that I'd seen the outside of this place, I'd think that I was in some run-down castle. This place needed some serious work and whoever decorated and configured the inside definitely needed to rethink their choice of career.

Chapter 32

Raios

I held my breath and pressed my back to the wood paneling of the door. Half of me had the sense to want to turn tail and find an excuse not to show her the room. What if she hated it? I did have a good sense of what she needed and what she liked, but still. I had never done anything like this for someone before, but I wanted to do everything for her. I wanted her to love her life here, to find joy here that she couldn't before and I knew I could make it happen for her.

I could fix her.

"Are you going to show me, or is you standing against the door the surprise?" She raised an eyebrow.

Damned to Hell, I was falling for this woman, and hard. Who knew such a strong feeling could manifest so quickly? I stared at her, soaking her in for all that she was. She stood before me; perfect arms folded across her even more perfect chest. That red hair of hers—so red it nearly matched my eyes—disheveled in the most endearing way.

"Hello?" She waved a hand in front of my face. "Anyone there?"

I smiled at her, wanting nothing more than to take her in my arms and hold her until we became one, but refrained from doing so, of course.

"Now, if you don't like it and you say you do, I'll know if you're lying." I winked and turned the knob behind me.

She rolled her eyes and I pushed the door open a fraction of an inch then stopped.

"Actually, close your eyes."

She regarded me. "Really?"

"Really."

Reluctantly she obliged my request and lowered her lashes until they formed perfect, beautiful crescents atop her cheeks. I moved to stand behind her, placing my hands over her eyes for good measure, and she huffed.

"Alright, walk forward about five steps." We moved as one and I made sure to tap the door open the rest of the way with my foot. "And, open!"

My breath was stuck in my lungs as she opened her eyes slowly. I forced her thoughts from my mind, too scared to hear her criticism and how much of a failure this gift was.

She was silent. So silent sweat began to prickle along my hairline.

She hates it. She fucking hates it. I knew it. This whole idea was a mistake!

Behind her I ran my fingers through my hair, tugging at the strands with a mixture of defeat and embarrassment.

She turned slowly and when her eyes met mine, I nearly fell to the floor from the sight. Tears streaked down her cheeks and my heart fractured.

Oh Hell, she *really* hates it.

I reached for her, unsure what to do but desperate to make it right.

"Sweet one, I—I'm so sorry. I thought this—I don't know. I'm sorry. You hate it, this is awful."

It took everything in me to not fall to a crumpled heap at her feet and beg for forgiveness. Shame and embarrassment overtook me.

Chapter 33

Deer

This room was the most beautiful space I had ever seen. It was beyond perfect!

The floor had been layered with several plush, white rugs. The lighting far brighter and more modern than the rest of the place. I could hardly fathom that someone would put so much effort into creating a space like this for me. To say I was blown away, was an understatement.

Tears began to sting my eyes as I marveled at the space. The room itself was massive; each wall held no less than one fireplace roaring with fiery life... A couch sat in the center of the room beside a small, rectangular, white coffee table—*my* couch and *my* coffee table. I spotted my laptop on the small table, along with a neatly folded pile of all my blankets.

I couldn't have stopped the tears from falling if my life depended on it, I was speechless. This man that had just popped into my life created this space *for* me.

He brought home *to* me.

Raios was having a mental breakdown over this because he thought I hated it, but he couldn't be more wrong. This was single-handedly the nicest, most wholesome thing anyone had ever done for me.

Come to think of it, he's done and been more for me in the last day, than I feel anyone has been in years.

"Though I've only known you a short time, I feel I understand you intimately. Not your life but you, your emotions, your dreams, your aspirations," I quoted softly.

He looked at me, worry colored his cheeks. "What?"

"Though I've only known you a short time, I feel I understand you intimately. Not your life but you, your emotions, your dreams, your aspirations," I recited louder, pulling him to me so our bodies were lightly touching. "It's a quote."

I could feel heat rising to my cheeks. "It uh—it just fits." I waved a hand between us, feeling dumb for saying it out loud.

"Oh," he replied quietly.

"Raios, I love it." I swung my head to look directly at him. "I'm crying because of how happy I am. This is the most thoughtful thing anyone has ever done for me. It's perfect—beyond perfect. It's amazing."

His shoulders relaxed, but he still wore an expression of worry.

"Read my mind if you don't believe me. You've been so good to me, better than anyone has ever been to me in a relationship. That's what made me recite that quote—I know it sounds dumb or whatever, but it's true. I've known you for such a small fraction of time, but it doesn't feel that way."

Now it was my turn to run my fingers through my hair. There was so much I wanted to say, but didn't know how to. This softer than silk devil waltzed into my life and (quite literally) swept me away. One would think I'd be panicking or terrified for my life, but that wasn't even close to the case. I can see everything he says, he means with his entire being. I had no idea what he was like before me or how he acted, but with me he wore his heart valiantly on his sleeve.

"I know it's past my birthday, but this is the best birthday present ever. *You* are the best birthday present ever. All of this is a whirlwind of insanity, but if this is just a small taste of what it's like being yours—materialistic things aside—I would say I am the luckiest girl on the planet—and I don't know what I did to deserve having you in my life."

Raios was speechless, his worry from before washed away—replaced by shock.

"I firmly believe even without the deal and everything it brought with it, even if we were in a different lifetime where you and I were the same, our paths would cross."

"We *are* inevitable," he whispered slowly, as if saying the words too loudly would jinx everything.

"I'm going to pretend that sounds far less ominous than it does," I said, laughing.

"So, you really like it?" he asked, sheepishly.

"What do I need to do? Pry my brain out and plop it into your hands? I love it. I more than love it. It's beyond perfect, Raios."

He grinned at that and his worry-rigid body seemed to loosen. I reached for him, wanting to hug him, the amount he worried over such a small thing was endearing. As I wrapped my arms around him and felt his body relax further into mine, I couldn't resist but marvel at the simplicity of the action. This was our first hug—obviously not a groundbreaking milestone by any means, but it was a funny thought, realizing I had ridden his cock before even doing something as simple as this.

BOYFRIEND FROM HELL

I held the devil to me, and thought loud enough for him to hear.

I wouldn't mind spending all of eternity with you.

Chapter 34
Raios

We spent the following days fully enthralled in one another. Creating that room for her was the best decision, it truly opened her up and brought her a sense of comfort I didn't realize could be brought upon by (what I had deemed) invaluable objects.

The days were filled with answering her questions about Hell and its inhabitants—how people ended up here, if pets end up here, how demons came to be and what they are. We lightly touched on our childhoods, how they differed and what it was like for both of us growing up. After the last few days—I felt as if I had known her for a lifetime. I explained mortality to her and did my best to explain how, and why, I was immortal—though the best I could come up with was 'that's just how it is'.

We also had a lengthy discussion about how our anatomies differ slightly, and that there is no way she could get pregnant from my seed—that was a far more awkward (though very valid and reasonable) conversation. And that's saying something, considering it's competing with the moment I had to confess my virginity to her. I knew some of my flippant answers didn't fulfill all of her curiosities, and I acknowledged that, realistically, I *should* know more than I did. But growing up,

I had next to no interest in learning about the history of this place or its people. Granted, I still don't—I've more or less succumbed to the fact that, regardless of my wants, I'm meant to fulfill a role of destiny and take over the family business of running the Underworld. But I digress.

"Raios?" My sweet one said, pulling me from my thoughts. I looked at her and gave a sheepish grin.

"I'm sorry—what were you saying, love?"

"I need help choosing a color for the hallway walls." She gnawed at her bottom lip.

I noticed she did that when she was either deep in thought, or weighing her options. It was a small thing I had picked up on instantly and I was glad she wasn't aware of the habit because she would surely attempt to stop the adorable quirk. I tilted my head to the side and examined the four, extremely similar, colors that were pulled up on her laptop—all of which were damned near the exact same shade of beige. Good thing Hell had no shortage of contractors, because there was no shot I was doing this solo. I'd have to send Mal or Cam topside to grab the things we needed—unfortunately *Home Depot* hasn't made its way down here—yet.

"Hmm," I hummed, leaning over her and the cozy little nest she'd made for herself on her couch. "I like that one."

"Really?"

She looked up at me, her face screwed into a look of distaste. I couldn't help but chuckle. I had settled into the realization that I loved her shortly after our 'date' in the Gluttony district. Every small thing she did felt like taking a bullet straight to the heart—and I welcomed each one with open arms.

For once in my bleak life, I had found my flame. "Oh, no, not *that* one?" I cringed, "Sorry, I actually meant *that one*." I jutted my chin aimlessly toward the screen and was rewarded with an eye roll and a haphazard swat in my direction.

"Choose whichever color you like, love. This is your home now too. I couldn't care less if the entire estate crumbles to the ground, so long as I have you by my side."

I planted a kiss atop her dark red hair, now haloed with black roots and streaked with gray. My star kissed, little nightmare.

Chapter 35
Deer

O ne Month Later...

Faux sunlight shone down on me as the sunset bulbs Raios installed grew brighter. I rolled over and smiled at the horned man curled beside me.

I was amazed at how much he had gotten done—painting, updating, everything. He even managed to get me Wi-Fi down here. I had no idea how *that* was even possible and I wasn't going to bother asking him either—despite how amazing he was, he truly didn't know much. I smiled at the thought, he was so goofy.

One would think, based on looks, that he'd be as rabid as a rottweiler or something of the sort—but he was softer than butter. I adored how transparent he was with me about every single thing. He didn't feign knowledge or boast about nonsense the way typical men often did. He was completely comfortable with who he was—at least around me.

Raios rustled beneath the covers and opened his eyes, giving me a sleepy smile.

Today was the day we were supposed to consecrate our bond. Raios spent the last week explaining to me what that meant and what it entailed. At first it freaked me the fuck out. I had imagined something akin to a wedding ceremony, or maybe some kind of announcement speech. Nope. We had to fuck in front of Hell and all its inhabitants.

Why? Because, according to Raios, that's just how things are down here—and how they've always been. It was an obscure tradition, but if you closed both eyes and tilted your head, maybe it made sense—maybe? (*Not really.*)

He explained it as a visual, intimate display of affection—us staking claim to one another. I don't know. I felt weird about it, but then again, this was Hell, and apparently, this was the only way for him to take his father's place as ruler.

Thankfully, his parents would *not* be present. Now that Raios was taking the reins of the theoretical—but also maybe not-so-theoretical—throne, his parents had been traveling a lot. Allegedly, Heaven was a great vacation spot this time of year.

"What's on your mind, sweet one?" Raios asked as he caressed my cheek.

He'd been doing great with not reading my thoughts, at least so he said. If he was, he no longer made it apparent, which I appreciated all the same.

"Just...worried about today, I guess."

He propped himself up on one elbow, a spill of dark, sleep-tousled waves falling over his eyes as he slid his tongue along his lower lip before pulling it between his teeth.

"Worried the heavens will hear you screaming the new ruler of the Underworld's name?" He smirked.

I batted his arm. I was worried about having sex in front of a bunch of people.

"If that's what you're worried about then hellfire forbid you ever stray into the Lust district."

Smokey shadows began to swirl around his palm, the icy tendrils pulsed between my cheek and his hand and I followed his eyes to the foot of the bed.

Mal and Cam appeared, wearing nothing but cream-colored linen boxers. Both had erections pressing firmly against the fabric.

My eyes widened and my breath hitched. It felt wrong to stare—but the size of the bulge barely concealed behind both of their shorts was impossible to ignore. They were both a part of Raios, right?

Raios wiggled out from beneath the warmth of the comforter, and I whined at his movement, watching as he strolled lazily toward the twins. The three of them exchanged glances—some kind of silent conversation passing between them—before all three turned to look at me with matching devious grins.

"What?" I drew the word out.

The three of them looked awfully suspicious, gathered at the edge of the bed, deep in whatever silent chat they were having. I didn't care for the sneaky grins they wore either.

I narrowed my eyes at Raios.

"What are you up to?" I asked as I sat up.

Raios put his arms around his shadow minions. "You're nervous about putting on a show for the Underworlders, so I figured a little practice might help."

He pulled his lower lip in between his teeth as his grin grew into something feral and hungry.

What the fuck does he mean *practice might help*?!

Cam and Mal separated, each creeping along either side of the bed, boxing me in. I eyed Raios nervously as the two men crawled onto the bed, each one taking up space beside me.

Raios continued to smile at me, and I couldn't help but wonder—*am I about to have a foursome with some shadows?*

Cam wrapped an arm around my shoulder; his cool skin was a stark contrast to Raios' warmth, and I couldn't help but shiver. My eyes stayed locked on Raios as Mal slid a hand beneath the covers and found the top of my thigh.

My breath snagged in my throat, and a familiar buzz of warmth began forming between my legs.

"You just tell me if you'd like to stop, or if anything makes you feel like this is too much, sweet one," Raios said tenderly., "I want you to feel comfortable and ready for later."

My heart throbbed at the consideration behind his words—my pussy also throbbed as Mal's hand snaked its way further up my thigh.

"They're extensions of me, you're safe," Raios reassured, with a sly smile.

"Ar—are you going to join?" It felt dumb asking it out loud, but it also was a very valid question.

He shook his head and waved at the twins as if gesturing for them to begin.

My heart was pounding in my ears, and I could feel myself growing wet with anticipation and curiosity. I'd never done this before—shadow twins aside—I'd never been with two people, let alone two people and *another* person watching.

Cam leaned into me, lowering his head to the crook of my neck and tracing the tip of his tongue along the column of my throat. I allowed my eyes to flutter closed at the sensation. At the same moment, Mal's fingers found their way to the edge of my underwear.

"That's it, my little nightmare." Raios praised me from the bottom of the bed. "Open yourself up to them. To me."

Mal curled his finger beneath the slim strip of fabric that covered me, his cold knuckle brushing ever so slightly over my clit. I couldn't help but spread my legs further for him. Cam latched onto my neck, swirling his tongue against the sensitive skin and nipping between sucks. If I weren't already in Hell, I would have thought I'd died and gone to Heaven.

I let my head fall back against the plush pillows cradling my back as Mal slid a finger along my wet slit. I groaned and spread my legs even wider, my clit throbbing with need.

Just as Mal slid the tip of his finger inside, Cam bit down on the soft flesh of my neck, and my back arched against the dual sensations.

"That's it, nightmare. Let my shadows pleasure you," Raios purred from somewhere in front of me.

There was a yank of the blanket, as if he was starving to watch what was unfolding before him. He pulled the covers from my body, exposing me to the open air.

A blush crept up my face—this felt so intimate, and it was hard not to feel self-conscious—but I swallowed the insecurity down.

I needed to do this.

I *wanted* to do this.

Cam reached down and tugged at the band of my underwear, easily tearing the thin fabric from my body in a quick, painless movement. Wasting no time, his fingers found my clit and began to rub the throbbing spot in small circles just as Mal curled his icy finger deep inside me, immediately finding that perfect spot hidden within me.

I croaked out a moan that was cut short as a mouth covered mine—I had no idea whose, did it even matter? Their tongue slid along mine as if they were trying to consume the moan that was fighting to escape my mouth.

I needed to grab something, *touch* something. The urge to feel one of their pulsing cocks in my hand surprised me as I pawed blindly around with both hands.

Grabbing hold of both men's throbbing cocks, I could almost salivate at how hard they were. Were they this erect for me?

"Of course they are, sweet one. You are the most divine thing to have ever entered Hell. They are no different than me in yearning, their lust for you mimics my own," Raios panted as I cracked open an eye to glance down at him.

It was a shock to find him fully nude standing before me, his cock straining against his brash grip as he stroked himself slowly to what was happening before him. The tip of his cock glistened and my mouth watered as I thought of how good it would taste to lick that glimmering bead from his tip.

"I feel everything they feel," he panted as he gripped his cock even tighter, causing the tip to turn pink. "Fuck, Deer you are perfect."

He reached down and cupped his balls, and began stroking himself hard, and slow.

"I can feel that throbbing, needy, soaked cunt of yours wrapped around Mal's finger," he panted. "I can feel your perfect fingers, wrapped around their cocks as if they were my own. I feel it all."

New motivation coursed through me at this fun fact. I squeezed the two men's cocks harder, a trio of moans erupting around me. Their cocks twitched in my grasp, and I let my head fall back once more.

Cam growled against my neck and bit me again as he applied more pressure to my clit. With Mal's free hand, he took mine in his and plunged it beneath his linen boxers. He growled as I gripped his icy cock and slid my thumb along the tip, collecting the pre-cum that spilled from it and swirling it around.

His paced quickened as he plunged a second finger into me and began fucking me with both of them. His movements were hard and fast, just on the border of being uncomfortable and euphoric.

"That's it, love," Raios' voice came out as a rough grunt.

I slid my other hand under Cam's waistband, gripped his cock, and began pumping both in tandem, keeping pace with Mal's fingers inside me.

Cam's movements on my clit relented for a brief moment as both men grabbed hold of my legs right behind the knee and lifted them up so the tops of my thighs pressed against my nipples. I was fully exposed to Raios in every sense of the word.

"Fuck!" Raios bit out as I felt a shift in pressure on the edge of the bed.

The pleasure I felt was all consuming, and it was lost on me how Raios—who was feeling quite literally triple of what I was, was able to even speak coherently.

I was sprinting toward climax and I could feel every part of my body beginning to sweat.

There was another uneven shift in weight on the mattress, as though Raios was trying to fight through the walls of pleasure.

Cam and Mal also shifted around me but I couldn't be bothered to do much more than what I was currently doing. My chin was tilted up toward the ceiling, my mouth opened in silent moans as my own pleasure from the two shadows swelled around me.

My shoulders burned from the vigorous strokes, but no part of me planned to stop. Each time I felt their cocks' jerk in my hands from the pleasure I was giving them, every grunt and groan that escaped the twins' lips, was fuel to the fire that was burning in me.

I knew the pleasure I was giving Raios was unfathomable, and the power that knowledge gave me made me deliciously greedy.

The pressure and fiery heat against my sides surprised me, and my eyes snapped open—Mal, Cam, and my hands never relented. When I opened my eyes, Raios was hovering in front of me, his cock just inches from my face. Sweat poured from his forehead as he pressed his free hand against the wall to keep his trembling body stable.

"Open," he moaned so softly that I was sure I was going to cum right then and there.

I peered up at those lust-laden, rose-colored eyes and parted my lips for him. Not wasting a single second he rubbed the glistening, wet tip along my lips. I stuck my tongue out, greedy for a taste. The moment his cock brushed against the wetness of my tongue he shuddered. The entire bed trembled from it as he plunged his cock deep into my mouth without a second thought. I gagged as I worked to coax my throat into relaxing.

Cam and Mal began to swear around me as one of them shifted. I had no idea who—Mal, I assumed based on the fact that, for a moment, the euphoric finger fuck he was giving me relented, as well as the fact that my hand was short one cock for a breath.

The tip of a cock brushed against my pulsing opening; it was as if my pussy was begging to be filled. Could shadows cum? Regardless, I wanted to feel that throbbing cock buried deep inside of me.

My best guess being that it was Mal—pressed his way into me, Cam never missing a beat as his slick fingers continued circling my clit.

I moaned around Raios' cock and I swear he began cursing in tongues. All three men's cocks began twitching feverishly and I knew they were all close. Thank God, because I had been suppressing my own orgasm the best I could the entire time.

I relaxed and let pleasure consume me as Raios fisted the back of my head, fucking my mouth like his life depended on it. Tears and saliva streaked my face, but I didn't care. I clenched around Mal's cock, savoring the way his cold member felt deep inside me, and gripped Cam's cock harder.

Mal was the first to break. His moan shook the room as icy cum spilled deep inside me.

Well, that answered that.

Cam had snuck his way back to my neck and bit down so hard there was no doubt I was bleeding. Cold strands of cum spilled from his tip, coating my hand.

Mal continued his pace as pleasure crept up from my toes and spread throughout my body, completely consuming me. The strongest orgasm I'd ever experienced crashed through me, and I screamed around Raios' cock. The vibration must have sent him over the edge.

A loud crash sounded above me and what felt like small particles rained down onto my face as Raios' body convulsed over me and his cock hit the back of my throat. Hot cum poured into my mouth and down my throat as I fought to swallow it all. His grip on my hair loosened and turned into a gentle stroke.

Time seemed to stop, all four of us vibrating at a frequency that could only be described as pure rapture.

Chapter 36

Raios

"How are you feeling, my love?" I asked, not wanting to poke around her mind. I drew lazy circles along her bare back as her head rested against my chest.

"I feel like as long as I have you, I can do anything."

Her voice was small and timid, but her words buzzed through me. Taking her chin between my fingers, I tilted her face up so I could look into her heartbreaking eyes.

I scanned them and found nothing but pure, serene contentment. Briefly, I peeked into her mind—more so for my own reassurance than anything—and found no traces of heartache. Her past had been eradicated and the only thing that filled her mind was me, and our future.

I smiled down at my heart in the flesh.

"Do you feel okay about the ceremony?" I asked.

She nodded and gave me a tired smile.

"As long as we are together, I feel like I could walk through fire and fight all the demons in hell."

I choked out a laugh, not expecting that response, and planted a kiss between her eyes.

"Take a nap, sweet one. We have a few hours until the ceremony."

"No freaky countdowns," she mumbled and nuzzled into my neck.

I chuckled. "No *freaky* countdowns."

I waited a few moments for her breathing to slow, signaling she had fallen asleep.

Closing my eyes, I thought back to her first moments here—my anxieties and worries pouring through Cam and Mal as they frantically got her ready for our dinner date... the same dinner my parents just so happened to crash. With that thought, I let my mind drift off to sleep. "I love you, Deer. From this life into the next, may our souls always be destined to intertwine."

Chapter 37

Deer

I was dressed in white silk that hung scandalously from my body, leaving very little to the imagination. With every movement the fabric brushed against my nipples, instantly making them hard. I grimaced at my reflection, self-conscious thoughts threatening to push their way in.

"Devastating," Raios whispered from behind me and my soul buzzed.

I turned on my heels, the reflection of him not doing him justice.

His suit was made of silk so black it looked as if the fabric was pulled from the night sky itself. It hugged his frame perfectly. Just tight enough to curl around his muscles, but not tight enough to reveal anything in particular.

The opposite of my outfit.

My eyes trailed over his body, starting low and slowly working their way up to his face, shrouded by tousled waves that fell around his horns.

I snorted. "Did you shine them?"

His eyes widened and a blush spread across his perfect cheeks.

"What?" His hand flew up to his horns and he squeezed his eyes shut. "Shut up!" He laughed and covered them with his hands.

I couldn't help but howl with laughter.

"You're too cute! Shining your little horns for the big show," I said in a baby voice.

He peered over his shoulder and flashed me a timid smile, rolling his eyes. Who knew the happiest moments of my life would be with the devil, in Hell.

"Are you ready, future Queen of Hell?" He lowered a hand from one of his horns and held it out to me.

"Let's show your—*our*—Underworlders who their new rulers are." I smiled through my nerves and slid my hand into his.

We stood atop a large stone cliff—which was far less intimidating than I thought it would be, given I was under the impression we'd just be fucking in the middle of a room with every one surrounding us.

Nervously, I looked up at Raios as he looked down at me.

He stooped down and knelt before me, and kissed the mark of our bond on my chest.

"You and me?" he whispered.

Was he nervous?

"You and me," I echoed.

He rose, releasing my hand, taking a step toward the edge of the cliff before throwing his arms out wide.

Below, the mix of unfortunate souls and demons howled and screamed for their new ruler. He waved a hand behind him, beckoning me to join.

I stepped up to his side and he took my hand once more, joining our fingers and raising them into the air.

The Underworlders screeched twice as loud, and I couldn't help but smile at the acceptance.

"Are you ready, sweet one?" He smiled deviously down at me, between our arms, and I nodded.

"Just, right here?" My throat was dry.

"Just right here, baby. It's okay. It'll be quick." He winked.

Hand still held high in the air, we turned to face each other. He took his free hand and cupped my cheek. I leaned into the warm, comforting sensation as he lowered his head and brushed his lips against mine.

He lowered our arms and placed my hand on his chest, while his free hand found the strap of my dress and brushed it off my shoulder. The flimsy fabric fell with ease, my breast immediately exposed. The crowd below hushed as the show began—it took all of my might, and confidence, to not cover myself.

"You're doing perfect," he whispered against my lips, as he palmed my breast and twisted my nipple between his fingers.

He stepped closer and pressed his hips into me. His erection pushed against me, causing my pussy to flood with desire.

I lowered my hand to palm his bulge; he hissed at the contact.

"So much for the virgin devil, huh?" I smiled against his lips.

He pulled away for a moment in mock offense, and flicked his hand against the dress, ripping it straight off my body. The hot Hell air caressed my skin and, in that moment, the only thing that mattered was the man in front of me.

He forced a hand between my legs and slid a finger along the wetness that he found between my thighs, groaning.

"So wet for me, little nightmare. Maybe you like the idea of this little show more than you've let on."

Maybe I did. Maybe I liked a lot of things I hadn't yet discovered, I thought to myself.

He pressed two fingers into my pussy and curled them toward himself with such force I staggered forward a step. I reached down with my other hand and placed it over his, pushing his fingers in deeper with my own and he growled.

A voice came up from below, a soft, confused yell filtered up through the hushed voices of the crowd. Raios began pumping his fingers in me and I quickly became enthralled with him and what he was doing.

I squeezed his cock harder and was rewarded with a growl so deep my pussy clenched around his fingers.

The voice from below grew louder and it almost sounded as if it was yelling—no, it was screaming my name.

"Looks like you've got yourself a fan, little nightmare." Raios panted against my lips.

"Deer?" The voice called out hoarsely and my curiosity got the best of me.

If I had a fan, maybe a little eye contact would push them over the edge. A little gift, if you will.

When I turned to look over the edge of rock, I scanned the crowd of bodies for the source of the yelling. A few rows in, frantic hands waved above the heads of others—and when I saw who they belonged to, my breath hitched and I froze.

"Little love?" Raios murmured against my lips, cock throbbing in my hand.

The color drained from my face.

That voice—I knew that voice.

His voice.

About the Author

Sedona Jessie is a dark fantasy author with a love for sci-fi, creepy creatures, and bite-size novels!

Her passion for writing began when she was in high school, where she would stay up far too late to watch anime. She'd spend countless hours writing stories in journals throughout high school, until she got her hands on her first laptop. Now, she still does the same thing—staying up far too late watching anime (but at least it's all streamable now) and pecking away at her keyboard, creating worlds.

When she is not creating, she can be found covered in her cats—Ned, Avocado, Noot, and Magnus.

Keep up with Sedona on Instagram - https://www.instagram.com/literarysedona/